Guelph Mercury Rising

Edited by Phil Andrews

Vocamus Press, Guelph, Ontario

ISBN 13: 978-1-928171-46-1 (pbk)
ISBN 13: 978-1-928171-47-8 (ebk)

Vocamus Press
130 Dublin Street, North
Guelph, Ontario, Canada
N1H 4N4

www.vocamus.net

2017

CONTENTS

Foreword

Phil Andrews

On the *Mercury*'s final day of production, a group of local citizens did something decidedly Guelphish.

As toonie-sized snowflakes fluttered down, they staged a flash mob-style hug of the *Mercury* building. The crowd offered many more hugs in the minutes that followed. Plenty were doled out to reeling members of the newspaper's final staff who were just hours from sending out their final edition.

The unplanned farewell function evolved. *Mercury* employees came to stand on the small, raised, front stoop of the Macdonell Street site and in an adjacent and fallow flower garden box. This happened while a few speeches were offered: about the moment that was unfolding and the era that was ending.

I was among the speakers. I struggled mightily and emotionally in doing so. I was moved by many things: the crowd; the pride I had in what the team that I was part of had delivered for years; the end of a part of Guelph for a hundred and forty-nine years.

I was also quite jarred and warmed by the many faces that came to be part of the crowd – very much including those of former *Mercury* staffers. There were former pressmen, reporters, newspaper carriers. Several I knew. A great many I had never seen before.

That's where a seed was planted for me. There is a wide, deep and proud community of *Mercury* alumni. A sizeable Facebook group has even popped up just among this unique family.

Months later, I had a crazy notion to try to have this crew unite for a special project to reflect its strength and spirit. I knew many members of the group had dabbled at writing fiction, on the side, for some time. I wondered if they could provide a compilation of short-stories for a book to emerge a year after the closure of the paper. The blue-skying included a working title: *Guelph Mercury Rising* and an ideal charity to back if the thing ever came to be sold. That was Action Read Community Literacy Centre. It had been a charity of the *Mercury* and an agency supported by volunteer efforts of some of its staffers.

Very fortunately, Jeremy Luke Hill, of Vocamus Press, saw merit in this fanciful idea and agreed to publish it – if I could get the Mercury Alumni Writers' Group to serve up enough stories. He had one more caveat. He insisted that I also have the contributors each offer a mini-bio to run with their offerings summing up their *Mercury* service and describing what they have engaged in since. I think that additional feature will be appreciated content by former *Mercury* readers who pick up this book.

The call-out for alumni contributions was met very favourably by the *Mercury* diaspora. Very little cajoling was required to have a contingent of compelling writers and these quite dear though very varied people provided an array of fictional offerings. (Please note, however, Alex Migdal's submission is a true story, and Magda Konieczna's offering is something like a one-act play. What can I say? Herding newspaper folks is something akin to doing the same thing with cats.)

Being engaged in the project brought back a lot of great memories for me. Newspapering is special, taxing, under-appreciated work. But, if it's for you, it's incredibly rewarding and very difficult to break from – particularly if that comes about suddenly.

Jeremy Luke Hill suggested the book might find appeal in Guelph because the daily paper never had a formal goodbye ceremony and because it was an element of thousands of local households for so many generations.

I hope *Guelph Mercury Rising* is well-received by the many supporters of the Mercury who have been so kind to the alumni group's members since the paper ceased its operations.

Thank you to the contributors. Thank you to Vocamus Press. And, thank you to the team at Action Read for the important work you do in promoting literacy.

My apologies to Metroland Media and to Ray Bradbury for sampling from the titles of the *Guelph Mercury* and *Mercury Rising* in generating a name for this book. And, my apologies to any members of the Mercury Alumni Writers' Group if you were missed in the call-out for submissions. If there is an ample volume of other offerings available, maybe a way can be worked out to see them get published in the future.

Phil Andrews
Guelph Mercury, Managing Editor 2005-2016
Editor, *Guelph Mercury Rising*

The Harbinger, 1983

Laura Lawson

The visits had been happening since she was a child, and for as long as she could remember, the creatures around her had always been harbingers of change. They brought with them warnings of what was to come. Their messages, always communicated in some strange, roundabout way, grew stronger and more frequent as she got older.

The summer she turned twelve, when the late August drought ravaged the land, large and industrious ants began to appear in the rental she shared with her mother and brother, Charlie. At first, it was just the odd scout trailing around, but soon others appeared on the same invisible trail. She was fascinated by them and watched their antennae twitch erratically as they navigated the kitchen in search of food.

"There's another one," her mother said in the most exasperated way, as she hit it with a fly swatter.

"Don't kill it," Sammie protested.

"I am not going to live with ants in my house. I've already got enough on my plate," she said, tossing the fly swatter and leaving the kitchen only to return with a 1970s Electrolux that had been a wedding present.

"You can't just vacuum them up," Sammie said. But that's just what she did, for each and every ant she found, until one day they returned from a trip to the grocery store and found hundreds of ants swarming a jar of honey on the counter.

"Who left that out?" her mother shouted, glaring at Sammie and Charlie. "That's it. I've had enough."

The exterminator came the following day. Sammie watched him as he cut holes in the baseboards and sprayed a fine white mist beneath the kitchen cupboards.

"That should take care of any carpenter ants living under there," he said. "But it ain't gonna solve your problem. You need to find the nest."

Three weeks later, after countless ants ended up in the black hole of the vacuum, the nest was uncovered. The ants had burrowed into the wall behind the toilet. A leak, likely undetected for years, was the apparent cause. The water had seeped beneath the linoleum and into the wall cavity, creating the perfect nesting grounds.

The exterminator returned and chipped through the damp floor boards and drywall, revealing black wood the consistency of Swiss cheese. As he tapped the boards, ants began pouring out in droves, each carrying an egg on its back the size and shape of a grain of rice. Sammie's mother screamed as the insects scattered across the bathroom floor.

And that was it, different this time than it had been before. But Sammie felt it: a sinking feeling in her stomach, the life being sucked out of her. She knew something bad was coming, and it couldn't be stopped.

It didn't happen immediately, although she spent the next three weeks on edge. She'd wake up in the middle of the night, hearing a phantom phone ring or the imagined voice of her mother calling out. School returned in September. During her walk home in the afternoon, Sammie dragged her feet looking for ants emerging from sidewalk cracks and sandy mounds along the pavement. She imagined them swarming bus stops and street signs, climbing over top of each other as they had done with the honey. When she closed her eyes at night, she saw them cascading out of the bathroom wall like a menacing black waterfall.

"It's a phobia," her mother said when she finally worked up the courage to tell her. "Don't you see? You're obsessing about the ants. They're gone. You don't have to be scared anymore."

"I'm not scared," Sammie said. "I just think…there's something to it. I have a feeling."

"What kind of feeling?" her mother asked.

"Like something bad is coming."

"Well, maybe if you stopped thinking about the ants so much you wouldn't feel so bad," her mother said, turning into the kitchen. "No more ant talk, okay?"

What Sammie didn't realize, and could hardly remember for that matter, was that this wasn't the first time she'd been visited. As a child, there had been others, disguised in fur and feathers, who always hid their true forms. The message they brought with them, communicated in various ways – through the bite of a dog or the murmurations of starlings – was always the same: Be careful, child. The world is not always what it seems.

It was only now, on the cusp of adolescence, that she was beginning to see a pattern. There were the mice that had scratched and gnawed in her bedroom walls for weeks until the day her father left. Never once did they show themselves. When she told her mother about the noises keeping her up at night, her mother grabbed a glass from the cupboard and placed one end on the wall and pressed her ear to the other. She expertly moved it up and down like a doctor with a stethoscope, listening for signs that things were awry.

"I don't hear anything, baby. If there's anything in there, it's gone now," she said, tucking Sammie back into bed. "Try to get some sleep."

But within moments of the door latching, the scratching returned and began to get louder. She could hear it over the shouting coming through the wall she shared with her parents. Sammie covered her ears and pulled up her blanket. In the blackness, she concentrated on the sound of her breathing, each breath longer and deeper than the one before it. After what seemed liked hours, she finally drifted off to sleep, her hands sliding gently from her ears to the pillow.

When she woke up the next morning, her mother was sitting at the table smoking a cigarette and staring at the back of a hydro bill. The ashtray on the table was overflowing.

"Where's Dad?" Sammie asked.

Her mother stood up and turned around sharply. In her haste, she dropped the bill, which landed in the middle of the table. I'M LEAVING. TELL THE KIDS I LOVE THEM. The writing was unmistakable: her father's.

3

"He gone?" Sammie asked, panic rising in her throat. She could feel her cheeks burning and tears welling up in her eyes.

"I dunno, honey," her mother said, taking a long drag off her cigarette. "I dunno."

Later that morning, her mother piled Charlie and Sammie into the Plymouth and drove two hours to the Rez. It had been more than a year since Sammie last saw Tóta. She looked older – the crevices in her forehead deeper, and the skin on her cheek softer. She offered a slobbery kiss and an exaggerated embrace as she greeted both children on the porch.

"Good to see you, Jeannie," Tóta said. "I was wondering when you'd be back. Hunter not come with you?"

"We need to talk."

"Sammie, Charlie, why don't you go gather some vegetables from the garden," Tóta said. "We'll have them for our lunch. Dig up some potatoes while you're at it."

Sammie threw her arm around Charlie and led him to the sprawling vegetable garden behind Tóta's house where green beans and runners of pea plants climbed up leafy stalks of corn. She instructed Charlie to hold his shirt out while she plucked sugar snap peas and placed them on the fabric.

"I don't want to carry them," he whined.

"Just take them into the kitchen and I'll start digging up the potatoes."

When Charlie was out of sight, Sammie wandered to the side of the house and peered around the corner at Tóta and her mother. They were deep in conversation on the steps of the wooden porch, Tóta's arm slung around her daughter's shoulder.

"You know you're always welcome here," Tóta said.

"I don't have a place here anymore."

"You'll always have a place here. This is your home. We'll talk to the Band. We'll sort it out."

"It's not up to them," she said. "I married out. And now what do I have to show for it? A bunch of broken promises and a couple of half-breed kids with no status."

"He can't take away who you are, where you belong."

4

"He already has," she said. "I've got no rights anymore. He didn't just leave. He took a part of me."

"Saaamie," Charlie yelled from the back door. "Saaamie, where'd ya go?"

Sammie disappeared around the corner and ran into the house. She watched from the kitchen window as her mother and Tóta walked to the car. They hugged, before her mother climbed into the Plymouth and backed out of the driveway.

"Where is she going?" Sammie yelled as she came running out of the house. "Where is she going?"

"Calm down. Your mother will be back. She's just going out for a few hours. Why don't we get started on lunch? Did you get the vegetables?"

Sammie stood on a step stool and helped Tóta peel the potatoes and wash the peas while Charlie watched cartoons in the living room.

"Your mother says you've been hearing mice in the walls."

"Yes."

"But she says she can't hear them."

"They're there."

"How do you know? Have you seen them?"

"No, but I hear them. She doesn't always listen the best."

"I know. Trust me, I know." Tóta said. "I hear them sometimes too."

"You do?"

"Yes. Your mother used to too, when she was a little girl."

"What is it?" Sammie asked. "It isn't mice, is it?"

"I don't think so. Not the sounds I hear, at least. But you need to listen to be sure. Even when you don't want to you. You need to listen."

"It scares me," Sammie said.

"You want to cover your ears? Hide from it?"

"Yes."

"Does it help?"

"No."

"We must face things head on, not run the other way. We can't see the wind, but we can feel it on our face. We can hear it when it's

5

gusting and know a storm is coming. We can't see it. We can't hold it. But its there, telling us something. But only if we listen."

* * * * *

Months passed and there no word from Sammie and Charlie's father. Rumours began to circulate, mostly on the Rez, that he had left for a white woman in Toronto. Despite Tóta's urging, nagging even, Jeannie remained resolute about moving her family back. She got hired on the lines at the Brown Shoe Factory. She worked a seven to three shift and then picked up the kids at school. For the most part, life transitioned to a new normal, though not without its struggles.

There came a point, about a year after he left, that Sammie stopped thinking of her father so much. It wasn't that she didn't miss him, she did. It was more that his absence became customary. She no longer thought of the spot at the dinner table as his, nor did she expect to see his work boots by the door. In a way, it was as though any mark of him was being erased. There were now only three inhabitants of the house. That is, until the ants moved in.

After the phobia comment, Sammie stopped telling her mother about the ants in her dreams, which continued to haunt her in both sleeping and waking states. She longed to ask Tóta about the heaviness she felt in her stomach, but she didn't dare mention it over the phone when her mother was in earshot.

Then, on a sunny but otherwise unremarkable Tuesday in September, the feeling disappeared. Sammie was in math class at the time, half listening to the teacher rattle off a lesson on Venn diagrams, when whatever had been burrowing through her let go. She stood up, relieved and disoriented, and turned to the classroom door. To her surprise, her mother was standing there, peering at her through the tiny window. She mouthed the word Tóta.

It took two hours to reach the hospital. Charlie wailed in the backseat from hunger and boredom while Sammie pressed her mother with questions: What was a stroke? Why was Tóta's brain bleeding? What did "critical" mean? Was she going to die? And there was one question Sammie didn't have the courage to ask: Was it her fault?

The sun was beginning to set as they parked the car and filed out. In the distance, Sammie could see the waterfront trail that snaked behind the hospital, its silvery birches and leafy maples cast in silhouette against an orange and pink sky. Sammie took a deep breath as she stared at the horizon. She closed her eyes and felt the wind brush her cheek and dance through her hair.

This time she heard it. It was faint, but not sad like she thought it would be. She knew that was to come, the hardship and fight. The feeling of being outside. But in this moment, it was filled with hope, like a bird finding its wings and then leaving everything it has ever known for good.

Laura Lawson landed at the *Mercury* as a cub reporter in 2006 and spent two years cutting her teeth on both the copy desk and municipal affairs beat. She left the paper in 2008 and moved into research communications at McMaster University. She is Mohawk (Turtle Clan) on her maternal side, and a member of the Mohawks of the Bay of Quinte. Her surname was Thompson when she filed her bylines for the *Mercury*.

Smithfield Ridge

Greg Mercer

The engine sputtered once, fired up and we pulled into the street. It was a bright, blue, cloudless day. At the top of the hill, you could see for miles – the seagulls circling over the mudflats, in front of oil tankers waiting for high tide, the dark green belt of trees that rimmed the city, the sun spitting its light on everything. We drove past a train bridge of rusty steel arches, a pulp and paper mill belching steam and a wide canyon rimmed by black cliffs holding back a churning river.

"Tide's still going out," Uncle Joe said, from the passenger seat.

He directed me to make a dozen turns, left and right and left and right, before we came to a neighbourhood of blockish, three-storey wood homes, looking like they had seen a hundred too many wind storms. They were covered in plastic and wood siding the colour of faded pants in a grandmother's drawer – nursing home beige, and spearmint green, and Easter egg blue. The houses ran in square, haphazard blocks, all hemmed in by empty streets where nobody walked and no cars drove.

"Indian Town," Joe said, at a dead intersection. "You should've seen this place when I was a kid."

"Where is everybody?" I asked.

Joe just smiled. He sent me down a street that ran parallel to the river. At the bottom of the hill, a cluster of tar-shingled warehouses were leaning toward falling down.

"I remember when you could take the streetcars all to the way to the bottom of the hill there. Then, the city killed those off, too. Decided we all should drive our own cars. You used to be able to come to the wharfs where they unloaded the fish. Then you'd get your hair cut right over there. For a dollar. Eel fishermen would hang their nets out in the street to clean them off, stringing them between those posts. You don't see that anymore. Anyhow, doesn't matter. We've got quite a ways to go yet."

We drove on with the river whipping by, leaving the city behind. Within the hour, we had left the highway and were driving a side road straight into the woods, the old Buick Cutlass rattling with every black patch of asphalt smeared into the pockmarked road. It twisted and turned like a logging route, the shoulder hidden by shoots of goldenrod that reached out in front of the car. I hadn't seen a road sign in miles. Joe was whistling along to the radio, another happy song about being a teenager and being in love and getting married.

"Up ahead, at the bend in the road, there's a little pull-over spot. Stop there," he said.

Soon, we were standing in a field of tall grasses, our shoes soaked from dew. Joe was looking around, mumbling to himself. Shaking his head. Cigarette nub in his leathery fingers, sending up grey ribbons of smoke.

"And over there, they had the schoolhouse. Spent a lot of time there," he said, pointing at a flat patch of land overgrown with alder bushes and small birch trees.

Joe began tramping around the field like a mad trapper, pushing his way through bushes and bulldozing past branches that scraped at my shirt. I stopped following him when a twig poked my cheek, hard.

"So. What do you think of Smithfield Ridge?" he shouted, from somewhere inside the thicket.

"Why did we come here again?" I said, rubbing the sting out of my face.

"Well. I figured it's a nice day and a good time to go for a walk. Thought you'd like to see the old Ridge. Two hundred years ago, this is where they all came. Just got off the boat from England and carved themselves a new life in the bush. Had everything they needed here. A post office, a general store, a blacksmith, even. They found their God's country, and never got the notion to leave. Just set down roots. Some called them backwoods people, but I don't know about that."

"I still don't understand why we're here."

9

"Well, we can't lie around inside all day, we'll lose our tans. The Cutlass needs to get out of the city from time to time, too, you know, just go for a rip on these country roads. Cars are like people, they need their exercise. And I thought you might like to see where your father grew up."

Joe's words bounced down across the grass and I spun around. On the horizon, a dark ridge of spruce trees were cutting into the sky. The field was gently sloping down toward the road, with a few big oaks standing on the hill. There was an abandoned farmhouse at the far end of the meadow, grey and bleached from the sun. The roof on a building attached to the back was collapsed and most of the windows had been smashed out. I thought about living here, but couldn't picture it.

"My father didn't live here. He was from Saint John. That's what Mom told me," I said.

"I'm sure she did. But this is where he grew up," Joe shouted. "Whether your mother would admit it or not."

"I don't know why –"

"Wait. Yep, I found it!" Joe shouted back.

I followed his path through the bushes and found my uncle standing over the stone foundation of an old building.

"This is the McKinley's house. Or what's left of it. McKinley was the farmer whose family owned damn near half the land out here. Most of the Sheppards leased land from him. Had a daughter, Ellie. She was something to see. Pretty near every boy in the Ridge was in love with her. Last I heard, she married some big-wig lawyer and moved to Connecticut. Oh well."

Joe nodded to a patch of cedars at the end of a dirt path overgrown with weeds. In the middle of it, a little wooden house was leaning badly, looking like it was propped up by the trees.

"That was Stan Sheppard's house, there. He was my dad's cousin, and he was the first out here to own his own truck. Your grandfather used to talk about going deer jacking in it, raising all kinds of hell."

"Why does no one live here anymore? They just up and left?"

"No reason to stay, I guess. They were country people, and the world just kind of changed around them. Their kids moved away, and when the old folks died, there was nobody left to keep the places up. Your father was probably the last one to leave. He was younger than the rest of us, so he stayed home longer. I think it was hard for him, being the last one. Mom spent her final years pretty much in bed, and Dad was never the same after she died. He just kind of had the life taken out of him. Waiting to die too, I guess."

"I've never heard any of this stuff before," I said.

"You're hearing it now," Joe said, spitting. His eyes were wet.

"He was a little hot in the head, your father, but he was proud of this place. It had a special meaning for him, more than most. I remember once, we were standing around after a hockey game in town and one of the guys was going on about Smithfield Ridge. 'Jeeze,' this guy said, 'Smithfield Ridge? You kick a stump and a Sheppard pops out.' Well, your dad just steps right up to him, gets within an inch of his face and says, 'One just popped out.' He wasn't but sixteen or so, and the guy just started babbling, saying he was sorry," Joe said, laughing hard.

He was looking at me.

"One just popped out," he said, shaking his head. "That's exactly what he said."

A bird was circling above the field, doing big, lazy loops through the sky with little twitches in its wings. It was one of those days, right out of a painting on some old lady's wall. I felt strange being here, like finding someone else's diary that you weren't supposed to read.

"Joe," I said. "Can we go home now?"

My uncle picked up a rock, turned it over and launched it into the bush. Then he started walking back to the car.

"You are home, kid," he said.

Greg Mercer is a New Brunswick-born, Guelph-based writer and national award-winning journalist. He's a reporter for the *Waterloo Region Record*, and formerly the *Guelph Mercury* (October 2005-February 2007), *New Brunswick Telegraph-Journal* and *Vancouver Sun*. He's also a contributor to Sportsnet.ca, the *Toronto Star* and the *Canadian Baseball Network*. His freelance articles have appeared in the *National Post, Ottawa Citizen, Edmonton Journal* and *Owl Kids* magazine.

Tagged

Deirdre Healey

Thursday

Alice can feel her heart pounding against the tree trunk as she watches him. Snot-nose Jason.

He is lying on his stomach on the pavement. His head is arched back and Alice can see a mess of gravel and blood covering his lips and the one side of his face. His eyes are squinted shut and two streams of snot glisten in the afternoon sun as they run from his nostrils down his bloody upper lip and into his gaping mouth. His crying overpowers all the other noise on the playground.

A feeling of satisfaction rises in Alice as she peeks from behind the gnarly trunk and she is unsure if she should embrace it or squash it. She doesn't like what she did. If she knew this was how it was going to have to end, she never would have played in the first place.

Monday (earlier that week)

At the sound of the buzzer, the line of Grade Four students shuffled from the classroom and down the hallway like a clumsy caterpillar of kids – toes bumping heels, chests bumping backs. It was lunch recess. The main event of the school day. Alice made sure to line up behind her best friend Jenna. She couldn't wait to tell her about the new jeans she was wearing. They had six pockets – three running down each leg – and there wasn't another pair like them.

The row of kids crumpled as it pushed through the school doors and poured out onto the playground.

"Let's play tag," shouted one of the boys before everyone dispersed. "Boys against girls."

Alice turned to look at Jenna to see if they were going to play and saw she was already running towards the soccer field where a tornado of students was forming. So Alice followed. It seemed the important jean conversation would have to wait.

The boys zig-zagged around the field with their arms outstretched trying to touch the girls. The girls let out a steady flow of shrieks as they struggled to stay out of the boys' reaches, but Alice wasn't among them. She was too fast for those out-stretched arms. Her strong legs bounded over the frozen ground as she ran circles around her classmates. No boy could touch her and she knew it. When she heard the thudding of feet coming up behind her she just told her legs to go faster and they did.

Eventually, the boys began to team up, coming at her from all directions trying to trap her. So Alice ran back towards the school. She knew the long chase would tire them out and she was right. Only one boy followed. Snot-nose Jason. Jason had joined the class a couple of weeks ago. He sat across from Alice. She spent a lot of time staring at him not because she liked him, but because he grossed her out. He always came to school with his black curls twisted into a patch of fuzz at the back of his head from lying on his pillow. He had dirt under his fingernails, orange stains at the corners of his mouth and a constant flow of snot running out of his nose. Alice nick-named him Snot-nose Jason, but kept it to herself. To the rest of the class he was just Jason.

With the school just metres away, Alice glanced over her shoulder to see who still hadn't given up the chase. When she saw it was Snot-nose Jason, she panicked and ran into the outdoor alcove of the school doors. With the doors in front of her and brick walls on either side, Alice had nowhere to run. Realizing she couldn't escape, she turned around to accept the tag. Only instead of an out-stretched arm, she was met with Jason's snot-nose face just inches from hers. He was so close she could see the tiny freckles peppering his nose and the roots of his thick black eye lashes curving up from his small dark eyes. His hands were pressed against the glass door windows on either side of Alice's shoulders trapping her and she could feel his breath repeatedly hitting her in the face.

"Now, I'm going to kiss you," he said with an orange-stained smirk.

Alice laughed nervously. Then, like in a game of Red Rover, she threw her body against her classmate's arms to try and push past him, but she couldn't break through. As he began to lean his head in close to hers, she shut her eyes and whipped her head back and forth, determined not to let him touch her with his mucus mouth. Her nervous laugh now silenced by her pursed lips. But it was no use. She felt his cold wet face press into her cheek. She had been slimed. Her body tensed in disgust. When Alice opened her eyes, Snot-nose Jason was already jogging back towards the soccer fields. She immediately scrubbed at her face with the sleeve of her coat, but it felt like her cheek would never be clean. Traces of that kiss would be stuck in her pores forever. She stood there scrubbing and swallowing hard, trying to push away the ache rising up in her throat. She had only wanted to play tag.

Tuesday

Alice wore her new jeans again today. She hoped she would get a chance to show them to Jenna during lunch recess. She wanted just the two of them to hang out on the playground and play hopscotch or braid each other's hair. As the class tumbled out the doors and on to the school yard, Alice did her best to stay close to Jenna. But just as she was about to reach out and tap her friend's shoulder, Alice felt someone push up against her back and sing, "I'm going to kiss you."

Her heart slammed against her ribs and she took flight across the pavement towards the soccer field. She refused to be slimed again. For thirty minutes, Alice ran and Snot-nose Jason followed. Alice could easily out-run him. She would sprint to the soccer field and rest until he caught up, or slow down her pace and jog around the perimeter of the pavement area, her brown pony-tail patting her on the back as she trotted. It was obvious Jason's legs were heavy, but he wouldn't stop the chase and worn a huge grin on his face the entire time . Alice wondered why he had decided to chase her. She didn't think she was the prettiest in the class. She had long, brown, straight hair that the girls liked to play with, but her face wasn't anything extraordinary – brown almond eyes, pale skin, with more freckles than she would like and thin lips that almost disappeared when she smiled. She was tall, taller than Snot-nose Jason, and thin. Too thin, she thought and was happily surprised when her new jeans fit around the waist. Maybe he was chasing her because of her new jeans, she wondered.

Alice ran past Jenna, who was sitting cross-legged on the pavement with a couple of other girls in their class, flipping through sticker books. Alice wanted so badly to be sitting with them. At one point she saw Jenna look up, her eyes followed Alice as she darted across the painted hopscotch patterns on the asphalt nearby. A flicker of hope ignited in Alice at the thought that Jenna might be able to help her fend off Snot-nose Jason. But then Jenna's gaze returned to the three-ring binder in her lap and stayed there.

Alice ran near the teacher on yard duty, hoping she would notice her. But each time she swooped in close, the teacher was bent over talking to one of the small children that swarmed around her feet like birds after breadcrumbs.

So, Alice spent the entire recess running. When the bell finally rang, she was standing by the goal posts on the soccer field watching Jason close the gap she had created between them. He stopped in his tracks at the sound of the bell, turned and started walking back toward the school as though he was punching out after a day of work. Alice waited until he was inside before following. She wasn't taking any chances of being caught between his arms again.

Wednesday

Alice spent another lunch recess running from Snot-nose Jason. She hoped he would move on from this game. But he didn't and began chasing her the moment she stepped outside. The playground was no longer safe. Recess was no longer fun. The wind cut through her ugly jogging pants and her hair kept slapping her in the face. Her arms and legs grudgingly did what they were told and there was a burning inside of her now. She hated him for doing this to her. For giving her no options. She couldn't stop or else she would be slimed. Yet, the thought of spending every lunch recess for the rest of Grade Four running away from Snot-nose Jason was unbearable.

At the end of the school day, Alice walked out of school alone. Usually, Jenna and Alice would wait for each other and walk down the hallway and out the doors together. But today Jenna walked right by Alice's coat-hook without even looking at her. Alice hadn't been able to play with Jenna again this lunch recess because of Snot-nose Jason and now she wondered if Jenna was mad at her because of it.

When Alice got outside, she saw her mother standing where the asphalt met the grass. Her hands rested on the stroller where Alice's little brother sat. Alice's mother always walked her home from school and today Alice was especially happy that she did. Her mother smiled and opened her arms as Alice walked right up to her and leaned into her puffy winter coat. Alice's body relaxed. She would tell her mother about Snot-nose Jason. Her mother would know how to stop him. As they made their way across the soccer field, Alice stared at the worn ground passing beneath her and listened to her mother rhyme off her daily list of questions. "How was your day?" "What did you learn?" "What did you play at recess?"

A heaviness filled her stomach when she heard the last question. Now was the time. But when she readied herself to speak, she couldn't find the words. She was suddenly unsure if it was something she should be telling her mother. She was unsure if she was doing something wrong.

"I played hopscotch with Jenna," came out.

And that was the end of that.

Thursday

At lunch, everyone was fidgeting in line waiting for the bell to ring; except for Alice. She stood still. The heaviness in her stomach weighed her down. She was tired yet alert, preparing for what would likely be another marathon of a lunch recess. She looked down the row of classmates behind her in search of the black curls and spotted him. She studied his face and scrunched her lips with disgust at the sight of the dried snot around his nostrils and the orange stains, which today were not only at the corners of his mouth but along his entire upper lip. Alice guessed it was orange pop. She thought about how her mother would never let her have orange pop for breakfast. Thinking about her mother made Alice regret not telling her about Snot-nose Jason. Now, she was forced to deal with him on her own.

16

When the class reached the other side of the school doors, Alice knew without looking back that the chase was on. She pushed hard past Jenna and the two other girls she was walking with. She didn't even turn to see if Jenna had stayed on her feet. She just ran and so did Snot-nose Jason. She took him to the soccer fields, past the row of trees at the boundaries of the school yard, back to the paved area and along the side of the school.

She looked back and saw the grin that was always spread across his face. The burning inside of her grew stronger. She felt powerful and in control. She could lead him anywhere she wanted. As she glided around, she could feel the sun's heat on her face – a nice balance against the crisp air. Today seemed more like fall than winter and all traces of the recent snowstorm were gone except for the thin layer of sand that had been scattered across the pavement to prevent kids from slipping on the ice. The grains crunched under Alice's feet and made her shoes slide slightly as she ran.

After taking Snot-nose Jason on a tour of the schoolyard, Alice slowed her stride and, like a pet dog, he caught up and ran right behind her. Alice didn't have to look back to know he was there. She could hear the scraping sound of his oversized shoes dragging along the ground. She hated how his feet sloshed around in his sneakers whenever he walked. Why didn't he get shoes that fit him? Why didn't his pop-for-breakfast-mother buy him a new pair?

The burning had now swelled from her chest. It flowed down her arms and up into her head. She looked across the playground at the sewer grate where the melting snow had left behind a pile of sand. She had run past it a dozen times already, but this time she sprinted towards it with purpose. Her feet were fast and precise, hitting the ground lightly so she wouldn't slide. Her chest tightened with nervous excitement and a burst of energy shot through her legs. She knew what she had to do. Without hesitation, her front foot landed hard on the grate, then her back foot. She pushed off the smooth metal and changed directions. Her feet slid slightly on the carpet of sand surrounding the grate as she picked up speed but she adjusted and kept going – the large oak tree in sight. As she ran towards it, she heard the long drawn-out sound of feet, then legs, then torso, hands and face sliding on gravel across the pavement. A loud cry shattered the icy

17

air. Alice grabbed the trunk of the tree with one arm and swung her body behind it. She was done running.

Friday

There was no snot and no orange stains, just bright white bandages. Half of Jason's mouth and nose and one of his cheeks were covered with squares of white gauze, framed with clear tape. Alice, who was sitting across from him trying to appear like she wasn't staring, marvelled at how clean he looked.

This morning was the first time Alice had seen Jason since she saw him sprawled across the sewer grate. She watched from behind the tree as the yard-duty teacher and her ballooning skirt of young children helped him up and brought him into the school. Alice didn't move from her spot until the bell rang and then spent the afternoon in class chewing on her nails and staring at Jason's empty seat.

A wave of relief washed over her when he finally appeared at the classroom door later that morning. As he walked to his desk, eyes followed him and whispers fluttered like butterflies across the room as kids volleyed questions and answers about what had happened.

Any relief Alice felt quickly faded when her thoughts turned to whether she would be in trouble over Jason's fall. But the morning dragged by without her teacher tapping her on the shoulder or the principal calling her out to the hallway.

Finally, it was lunch recess. The class lined up, just like it did every day, only today was a bit different. Alice noticed her classmates were gently jostling to stand next to Jason. She watched from the back of the line as a couple of boys patted him on the shoulder while Jenna, who managed to sneak right in front of him, was staring at his face and asking him if it hurt. In the midst of it all, Alice could see a half smile creep up Jason's good cheek. He seemed to like the attention.

Once outside and free from the restraints of the line, almost the entire class huddled around him, blurting out questions like a scrum of reporters. The loudest was Jenna, who yelled out, "Can you take off the bandage? We want to see what it looks like." Suddenly, kids started chanting: "Take it off, take it off." Alice stood on tippy toes a few steps back from the crowd. Her eyes glued to Jason. She too was curious.

Jason reached up and gingerly tugged at the tape. It was like watching him open a present. He slowly peeled off the square piece of gauze that was covering the one side of his lip. Underneath his lips were covered in a thin layer of pale yellow pus that spread from his bottom lip all the way up to his nostrils and continued under the bandage taped to his cheek. The skin beneath the pus looked a dark reddish purple, too fragile to be exposed. Alice sucked in breath at the sight of it. She was repulsed. And enthralled. She wasn't sure which was worse – this or the snot and orange stains. After a good look, she shifted her eyes slightly upwards and met Jason's eyes. He was looking back at her, softly staring.

All Alice could think about was the sensation of having those bloody, pus-oozing lips pressed against her cheek. Without willing it to do so, her arm brought her hand to her cheek and rubbed at the spot where he had left his mark. It had changed her. She didn't know how. All she knew was that she would never be the exact same Alice who had run toward the soccer field Monday afternoon to play with her classmates. She had been tagged. Alice broke her gaze with Jason and spun around on one foot. She sprinted towards the soccer field. She didn't know or care if he was following. She just needed to run.

Deirdre Healey joined the *Guelph Mercury* newsroom in 2004 after a couple of years reporting for newspapers in London and Woodstock. At the *Mercury*, she initially covered crime and later covered health and municipal politics. She left to work as a reporter for *The Hamilton Spectator* about three years later, where she covered breaking news as well as business. She later joined the University of Guelph in a communications and public affairs role. She stayed connected to the *Mercury* and its readers, however, through her weekly column Born and Raised. After the birth of her second child, she decided to leave the workforce, but maintained the column until the newspaper closed up shop. She currently fills her time with freelance writing and caring for three kids, which for now provides her with all the excitement she needs.

The Retreat

Declan Kelly

Martin watched his daughter Emma trace the edges of the marks in the grass with a stick from the winter debris they had raked from the lawn. Five months of snow and the spring rain had done little to conceal the deep ruts where the tow trucks had pulled the car back onto its wheels before dragging it onto the road taking it away. The spot was like a wound she needed to see again but dared not touch.

"Do they still talk about him at school?" he asked, knowing she would be thinking only of the accident and the boy.

"It had stopped for a few weeks," she said quietly. "But then on Friday, when they announced the tree planting ceremony for next week, that was all they were talking about."

"Have you made up your mind on where you want to go?"

She scowled slightly in response, and it made him feel insensitive for changing the subject too abruptly. He began raking and tamping a mixture of topsoil and compost into the dark grooves in the grass, straddling the unusually high runoff as he worked on either side of the ditch.

"I'm leaning toward McGill," she said. "But I haven't totally closed the door on U of T."

He liked the thought of her being in Toronto, if only to be closer to her. But he knew it didn't matter where she went, their time together was drawing to a close. She would embrace big city life wholeheartedly and not look back. At staff parties, his colleagues joked about being parents to the boomerang generation. But he couldn't see Emma coming back to the slower pace of their small hobby farm or the area in general. He had the slight consolation of knowing he would be one of the more prominent relics in her memories of a rural upbringing, but a relic all the same. He looked up to find her gazing at the base of the telephone pole where the boy's mother, Daphne, had attached a small white cross made of wood. Across its arms in the clean strokes of a fine brush she had painted: "JOHN McCORMACK 1993-2010 RIP." Below this she had attached the boy's last school photo and, toward the base, added "Love Mom." Martin had first noticed the woman's car a week to the day of the accident and then every Sunday for the past six months. If they happened to be driving out of or into the laneway when she was there, he and Emma would pull over and ask how she was doing.

"I hear the food's better at U of T," he said, smiling at Emma.

But as he turned to see her reaction, he noticed the woman's car pulling up to its usual spot. He was surprised to see her a day earlier than her usual Sunday visit. She got out of her car and asked if they minded if she dug a small flower bed, to mark the spot more properly. He said they wouldn't mind at all and offered to help.

"Thanks, but I think this is something I need to do on my own," she said.

"'Sure, of course," he replied and motioned for Emma to help him gather their things, and they walked back to the house in silence. He watched from the kitchen window as she first marked out and then dug the small rectangular bed before moving the white cross to the middle of it. The following Sunday, she added flowers that bloomed in cycles throughout the summer. In the fall, she cut the last of their withered stocks and replaced them with two large potted mums.

When he and Emma had washed up and shared a cup of tea, he suggested they go into town for dinner at the hotel. He was pleasantly surprised when she agreed. She was now at an age where being seen with your father on a Saturday night signalled a girl with nothing better to do, and no one better to do it with. In the car, he said nothing when she abruptly changed the radio station when the news mentioned some new procedure that was showing promising results in the early detection of breast cancer. He thought of Mary, naturally, but also of Daphne. It occurred to him that a major loss, whether of a partner, parent or child, brings about new rituals and taboos. When Emma left the dial on a station playing top 40 schlock instead of seeking out the indie roots rock she normally preferred, he knew it was something deeper. More evasive measure than teenage gloominess. Researching schools and now deciding where to go had been her entire focus lately, and to have that focus suddenly pricked by a reminder of her mother seemed to rattle her. Still, he liked that she was taking one of her first major life decisions so seriously. She was doing what was best for her, with little or no thought to what her friends were doing or what they might think. Every year at this time he would overhear conversations in the hallways of someone going to this or that school to follow a friend or romantic interest. But the closest Emma came to allowing personal interest a stake in her decision was saying that she was leaning toward McGill's poli-sci program because one of the main profs was a former international affairs reporter and was known to regale his classes with stories from his many foreign postings.

"While covering the FLQ Crisis for *TIME*, he had his typewriter seized by the RCMP,'" she had read to Martin from a student blog while eating cereal at the kitchen table the weekend before the applications were due. "It was a fucking typewriter! What did they expect…that they'd shake it upside down and find hidden stories that some foreign government would use against us?"

"Fair point," he nodded. "But ixnay on the uckfay in this house, if you don't mind." She met his ever-the-teacher-dad tone with a sheepish ever-your-loving-daughter look of regret and put a hand to her mouth. A blush cum *mea culpa* that put everything back into balance as only she could. He would miss that. It made him think again of the boy's mother. He felt self-indulgent, knowing she would easily swap places with him. He wondered what her life must be like now. From all accounts in the staff room, the boy had been her entire life. She had enrolled him in multiple sports, music lessons and exchange trips abroad. One of Martin's colleagues surmised it was a case of a single parent over-compensating for whatever was lost when the boy's father went to work in Fort McMurray and didn't return. He wondered if he wasn't guilty of that at times himself with Emma. Who could say how a person's parenting style might have turned out had things gone more according to script? He thought of this a lot now that Emma was weighing up which school to attend. It was as if her mother's death had spurred her on to pour everything she had into her final year and a half of high school. He wasn't surprised when she received generous scholarship offers from her main choices, U of T, UBC and McGill. But he noticed she had adopted a more casual air toward school since learning of her early acceptance. He put this down to having worked so hard for something and now, with the finish line in sight, she was looking beyond high school to a new phase in her life.

The previous fall and into the early part of the year, they had taken weekend jaunts to visit the schools Emma was considering. She arranged all the travel details and accommodation, surprisingly at a fraction of the price he had expected for each trip. In Vancouver, this meant staying in a clean but bare-bones room at the Y, with a shared and less than clean washroom at the end of a very long corridor.

In Montreal, they stayed at a B&B run by two former high school teachers from Ontario. The woman had taught French, but now fancied herself as chef of the manor, which was actually a faux Mansard walk-up near where the Habs played. The woman's husband had taught business, but was now trying his hand at painting. His large canvases were hung gallery-style throughout the house, with white title cards indicating the medium and price of each work. "Do you think he was going for abstract or just kind of missed the mark?" Martin had whispered to Emma when he saw her eyeing up the large canvas in their room. This was after they traipsed back from a nearby bistro in the snow, having drank red wine together for the first time, and Emma laughed uproariously. He would miss that too. How her laugh filled an entire room and even seemed to chase away the drafts in their old farmhouse kitchen.

In Toronto, they found no such quaintness and opted for a budget motel south of the St. George campus. But they did manage to have another great meal together at an Indian restaurant on Queen Street. When the red wine began to take hold on that night, he said that this would be known as their "Last Supper Tour" and joked about having t-shirts printed like the ones she had brought home from the concerts of her favourite bands. "I'll still visit, you know," she teased. "I mean I'll need to do my laundry somewhere." If only she would come home as often as she needed to do laundry.

She chose McGill in the end. "At least it isn't Vancouver," she said when he feigned disappointment that she hadn't chosen Toronto. In truth, it pleased him to think of her immersing herself in Montreal's old-world European vibe, though he suspected it was much changed since he and Mary had spent a weekend there before they were married. Emma confirmed as much in her first phone call home. No separation anxiety indeed, only talk of new friends and "the scene" in the Old Port, on the Plateau, and along Saint-Denis, where she had already found a job in a trendy café. "My apartment's a dump, but a super-cheap dump...and living off campus was totally the right call," she declared in her first email update. She phoned him every Sunday at first with the occasional midweek email. This soon faded to every month, which he put down to the demands of midterms and a glut of reading.

She returned home that summer to resume her landscaping job with the township and live rent free after having sublet her apartment. But the dynamic between them was somehow different. On weekdays, Emma was usually out the door just as he was hitting the shower. and after their unusually quiet suppers she generally stayed in her room. There, she would read, listen to music and mostly video chat with her Montreal friends until late into the night. He would hear the odd male voice, but didn't want to pry as he imagined Mary might have done. He didn't give it much thought until the following Christmas, when Emma sent a terse email saying she was staying in Montreal. "It feels more like home now," she wrote. "Hope you understand. Emm xo."

That February, she emailed to say she had become serious with someone, Jean-Franois or "Jeff", who was something of a renowned social justice activist. "All the main student unions are banding together to protest the government's ludicrous plan to increase tuition. Exciting times ahead!" she wrote, before signing off. He tried to sound casual in his response, but hoped she wouldn't take it entirely in jest: "Just remember our one rule from when you were growing up – no dying (and try not to get arrested)!!" She replied almost right away with only, "Ha! No need to worry about me. And, btw, that sounds like 2 rules. xo".

Over the following months, he followed the news from Quebec with greater interest, as the student demonstrations grew in both their size and increasingly militant overtones. On the front of one of the national papers, he saw a photo of a masked girl who bore a slight re-semblance to Emma. But it was small enough that he couldn't be sure. She held one hand aloft in a defiant fist while the other was helping to carry a banner that read "Printemps érable." He thought the nod to the uprisings that had taken the Middle East and North Africa by storm was a stretch in the extreme, but he imagined that leading large crowds in civil disobedience likely required a certain degree of hyperbole. He studied the photo intently and saw that all of the students holding the banner and hundreds more behind them had little red squares attached to their jackets and hooded sweaters.

As April ran into May and he hadn't heard from her in weeks, he knew she wouldn't be coming home that summer either. So he was surprised when he got a call from the owner of the café who sounded quite annoyed. Emma had given his number as a secondary contact when she started working there. She hadn't reported to work in over a week and he wondered if he should pull her name from the schedule. He told the café owner he was sure there was some good reason for it and said he would track her down and sort it out. He dialled her mobile and got her voicemail, which she now gave in English and French. He tried not to sound panicked, but he said her boss had called and he wanted to know that everything was OK. He followed this with a simple email, "Everything ok? Call me when you get a chance. Love D."

When she hadn't responded to either by the next day, he left an-other message on her phone, again trying not to sound overly con-cerned but hearing the worry in his own voice as he spoke. As he hung up he realized he had very few ways of checking up on her if he couldn't contact her directly. Apart from her first month or so at McGill, he had avoided looking in on her various social media profiles as it felt like eavesdropping on a conversation that wasn't intended for his ears. He caved and decided to look into her activity online. This yielded only a few blurry photos of her, either in demonstrations or having drinks in dimly lit bars with people he didn't know. More red squares pinned to sweaters, but no new posts in more than a week.

Two days later he heard his phone beep after midnight and opened it to find her reply to his email. "All's fine, but I'll be going quiet for a while, who knows how long. But please don't worry about me. A group of us have decided to break away, head for the hills and live off-grid. Love you xo Emm." He sat up in bed and called her straight away. An automated voice told him the number was no longer in service. He could barely steady his hands as he replied to her email. "Emma, Please call me!! Or I can come to Montreal or wherever you are, but we need to talk about this."

The next morning he called in sick to the school and contacted a friend with the OPP, who referred him to the missing person's office of the Montreal police. He hesitated before calling the number. But then decided that lodging a formal complaint would somehow confirm the absurdity of what he still believed to be a misunderstanding or even a prank gone too far. The officer took his story and asked for all of his Emma's details before saying that, as it appeared to be a wilful disappearance, his options were limited. But he said he had heard of a few offshoots of the main student demonstrators forming commune-style camps in abandoned rural cottages, and he promised to look into it.

When the officer hadn't called back two weeks later, Martin decided to make his own trip to Montreal and the surrounding area in the hopes of finding her or at least confirming where she was, and that she was there of her own volition. He visited the café where she had worked and spoke to the staff and anyone with a red square who would talk to him. At a table in a corner at the back of the long room, he thought he saw her. But when he approached calling Emma's name, the young woman turned and said angrily. "Emma, moi? Non," before laughing with her friends. Her laughter was shrill and cold.

A few weeks later on his next trip to Montreal, driving through one of the city's rougher neighbourhoods, he saw the face of another young woman aglow as she looked into her phone while she walked a scrawny dog. She was Emma's height and build, but he didn't need a second look to know it wasn't her. Unlike most of the kids at the school, Emma didn't need to know what her friends were doing at every waking moment. At big gatherings, she never felt the need to pretend to be checking her phone as most people do. If she wasn't directly involved in the conversation around her, she would merely look off into the middle distance. He remembered that serene look and the very thought comforted him and pained him.

When the missing persons officer called to say he had no new leads, Martin decided to head back to Ontario. As he drove, the international news was dominated by the Snowden story and the extent to which the NSA was listening in on private communication. He pulled the car onto the shoulder of the highway, turned off the radio and listened to the noise of the cars and trucks whizzing past. He began to attach a glimmer of hope to the idea that either a personal or group paranoia had had some hand in her "heading for the hills" in total radio silence. The independence and conviction he had long encouraged in her come back to bite him. He could do nothing else but hope that she would one day return to him and explain where she had gone and why, and why she had to break off all contact.

As he returned home from the fourth or fifth Montreal trip, his mind was a familiar blur of disappointment and regrouping, trying to rearrange these faint irons of hope in a flickering fire that only he tended. Just as he had continued tending to flower bed and marker at the end of his laneway despite the boy's mother not having visited in more than a year. He would use these return trips to constantly rework his scenarios of where she might be and why, only to realize he had travelled entire sections of the 401 without realizing it.

Now, as he crossed Toronto, the light snow that had been falling all day grew heavier and sudden gusts brought the traffic to a crawl. It didn't take long for the slower pace and now driving snow to lull him into a state of nodding and blinking hard at the road. Remembering there was little in the fridge at home, he pulled into a highway service station that was just before his exit for home. Even the line from the off-ramp to the parking lot was only inching along as most drivers sought refuge from the growing storm. Inside, the lines for the washroom and food counters moved just as slowly. But he eventually got some food and found a seat at a crowded corner table. As he settled himself, he looked across the aisle to see an unmistakable face, though it had aged in the years since he last saw it.

"Hi, Daphne," he began timidly. "How are you?"

"Why, Martin, what a thing to run into you here of all places," she said, as she rose from her seat and came across the aisle to see him. She asked the woman opposite him if she minded switching places.

"Dreadful weather out there, even compared to what we get up in the Soo," she noted, as she settled in at his table.

"Ah, is that where you've gone?" he replied "I wondered why you no longer stop by the house, well, the flower bed...you know."

She smiled at his embarrassment and explained that she had moved to Sault Ste. Marie last year when her brother-in-law had passed away quite suddenly and left her youngest sister with two young kids.

"And how is...it's Emma, right?" she asked.

"I wish I knew how Emma was," he began tentatively. He couldn't tell if her look of regret was at having asked or at fearing the worst. Either way, he saw no point in glossing over any of it and surprised himself with how he managed to describe how his only daughter had drifted out of his life, especially to a not-quite stranger who had borne her own unimaginable loss of a child. He started to wonder where he would put a marker to Emma's life and what he might include on it, before resolving not to entertain such speculations. He realized they had fallen silent for a few minutes, possibly longer. He imagined they were both trying to size up the other's situation, and doing so with a strange mix of envy and pity. It had felt good to speak of Emma in that way, openly but with whatever optimism he could muster.

They heard a sudden commotion and turned to see that the snow had eased and that many people were bundling up to return to the road. As they put on their coats, she said it was great to see him again.

"Despite the circumstances," she added. "I've learned that they never truly leave your life, whatever happens."

"Thanks," he said. "It certainly doesn't feel that way at the moment, but I'll try to remember that."

As she turned to go, he asked her if she would be stopping by the farm before she headed north again.

After a slight pause, she said, "I don't feel the need to stand there, at the very spot, as I did for those first few years...But thank you for taking care of it as you do – my other sister drove by it last summer and sent me a photo. It looks lovely. But I think, yes, I would like to see it again. If that would be OK with you?"

"Of course."

They made plans for coffee the following afternoon and made their way to their cars in the crowded lot. As they joined the queue for the on-ramp, they shared one last wave, and he followed her out into the night and the aftermath of the storm.

Declan Kelly was the *Mercury*'s arts and lifestyles editor from 2006 to 2009. After leaving the *Mercury*, he worked as a copy editor at the *Waterloo Region Record* before transitioning to communications and media relations roles related to public policy, research and post-secondary education. He still does occasional freelance writing on the arts, and has been published in *The Canadian Press*, *Grand Magazine*, *Macleans.ca*, *The Music Times*, *The National Post*, *The Stratford Beacon Herald*, and *Waterloo Region Record*. He lives in Stratford with his wife and son.

Safe Keeping

Chris Seto

The late August sun felt warm on Jake's face as he walked along the river trail by his apartment. Closing his eyes, he tilted his head up to let the sun's rays pour over him, letting his dog temporarily take the lead – he needed this walk more than she did.

Life was stressful. He loved his job and was happy to be working, but he always dreaded the approach of fall. It seemed like every year his employer celebrated the coming of autumn with a fresh round of layoffs. There were already rumours moving through the skeleton-staff at his office, whispers of the impending axe making a return in the coming months.

His relationship was also a source of grief. He and Samantha were both wonderful human beings, with shared goals and desires, but for the past year or so, they'd been like a couple of matchsticks dancing around a powder keg. Nearly every conversation sparked an argument that was fuelled by frustration and disappointment with where they were in life. These bouts were only suppressed when one of them left the room. That was what this walk was all about.

With every step he took, Jake forced himself to breathe a little deeper and pull his shoulders down away from his ears. The warm breeze moved slowly along surface of the river, keeping pace with the water. It brought him a sense of peace and helped clear his mind.

For a sunny Saturday afternoon the trail wasn't very busy, Jake thought to himself. This was fine by him. With a pull of the leash, he led Lucy off the gravel trail and through a break in the buckthorn trees to get to the water's edge. Slipping off his sandals he followed her into the cool water, letting the muddy bottom squish between his toes. The river was only about five metres wide and half-a-metre deep in the middle. The water wasn't very clean, but Jake didn't care. He waded out from the shore and let the leash go free.

"Dammit!" he said, stopping mid-stride as pain shot up from the little toes on his right foot. Reaching into the water, he felt around for the offending rock with every intention of hurling it into oblivion – or at least hucking it down stream. His fingers moved along the face of the object, searching for a way to grab it and bring it up. Finding nothing but a small hole to fit his finger inside, his mood shifted from anger to curiosity.

Now reaching in with two hands, he held his face near the surface to size-up the object. The silt on the bottom made it difficult to see through the water, but Jake was pretty sure he'd stubbed his toe on a piece of garbage. The object was square, smooth and solid, stretching about 40 cm across.

Maybe it was a mini fridge, he thought. He'd seen a lot of trash hauled out of this river over the years and there wasn't much that would surprise him. He was just about to move on when his fingers came across what felt like a dial on the face of the object.

"What the hell?" Jake muttered to himself. In the background, he could hear Lucy splashing around at the water's edge, playing with a crayfish.

The dial wouldn't twist – too gummed up with grit to move, Jake thought, but it made him even more curious. With a bit of hesitation, half expecting to run into a jagged edge and cut his hand open, he explored a little further and along the side of the box. Furthest from the dial, he grabbed what felt like a thick, bulky hinge. As the water moved downstream and cleared away the silt kicked up by his feet, Jake was able see the front door of the metal box through the brown haze.

Immediately he shot up from the water and looked around. No one was in sight. Lucy was enjoying herself, trotting back and forth along the shoreline. Making a mental note of where he was standing, he methodically moved backward towards the edge of the bank, counting his paces. Jake picked up a small stick from the shore and stuck it in the mud directly behind his left foot. Eight paces forward would bring him back to the spot, he thought. After surveying the tree line once more to memorize his location, he called for Lucy and made his way back to the trail.

* * * * *

His mind was racing when he got in the door. Drying Lucy's paws off with a grubby blue towel, Jake stared straight ahead. He didn't hear Samantha calling for him.

"Hello?" she said with an annoyed tone, sticking her head into the laundry room.

"Sorry, what?" Jake's gaze remained unmoved.

"I said there's nothing in the fridge and I don't feel like going shopping. Did you want to get Thai food tonight?"

"I found a safe." The words spilled out of his mouth much quicker than he intended. On his way back from the river, he promised himself he would keep his discovery quiet until he was able to open it, or at least drag it out of the water.

"I found a safe in the river. It's either a safe, or some kind of locked box, but I'm pretty sure it's a safe."

Samantha stepped into the room, head slightly tilted, her furrowed brow hidden beneath bangs.

"A safe? What are you –"

"I was walking in the water and came across this metal box with thick, beefy hinges and a dial on the face of it. I think it's a small safe. Like, the kind rich people would keep behind paintings in Bond films. It's underwater, half buried in mud, but I think I can get it out."

Samantha stepped forward as Lucy shot past her legs. With a hand leaning on the dryer, she locked eyes with Jake and opened her mouth as if ask another question, but nothing came out. She was going through the same thought process Jake had gone through on his way home, moving from confusion to realization of what this could mean for them, to plotting on how to bring it in.

What was inside it? It must be valuable, Samantha thought. You don't have a safe unless you're looking protect something important. Cash? Jewels? Bars of gold? In this neighbourhood, could be anything. Whatever it was, it could change their lives.

32

"I marked the spot with a stick. It's not far from the road. I think we could drag it out with the car," Jake said.

She nodded slowly, mouth still slightly open.

"We'll go get it tonight, when no one else is around. No one can know about this, Sam."

Still nodding, she sharpened her gaze with her partner and in a wordless glance, confirmed that she was on board.

* * * * *

The night progressed forward in relative silence. Thai food was ordered but little was eaten. For the first time in months, the couple cozied-up on the couch together and watched Netflix to kill time. They didn't pay much attention to what they were watching – their thoughts were firmly fixed on the contents of that box in the river.

As 3 a.m. rolled around, the pair left their small basement apartment, all dressed in black. This was Samantha's suggestion. They needed to retrieve their treasure without being noticed and dressing for the shadows would make it a little easier, she thought. And they did not want to get caught. Not with a safe. Not in this neighbourhood.

The pair lived in a small city, but it was no stranger to organized crime. For years the river by their house has been a notorious dumping ground for everything imaginable, from bathtubs to bodies. In the springtime, the water was fast moving and most items dropped into the torrent would be carried away. Whenever police enter into a missing persons investigation, one of the first places they searched was a deep pool of water downstream in a neighbouring township – a swimming hole known by locals as "Terminus".

Jake imagined the safe to have been stolen by a local gang and abandoned in the river during some sort of a raid. They will likely come back for it, he thought, but hopefully not tonight. Jake figured if the pair were caught retrieving it by the wrong people, they were as good as dead. But he was also a big believer in finders-keepers and saw the treasure inside this box as a way for the pair to escape the mundanity of their day-to-day life.

Stepping into their red SUV, the pair went over the plan – it was pretty basic. Sitting in the passenger seat, Jake rummaged through a black duffel bag to make sure they had everything they needed. An avid climber, Jake brought his sixty metre climbing rope, a couple of carabiners and a set of spring-loaded camming devices. These cams were normally wedged into a cracks on rock walls to carry a climber's rope, but they could serve dual purposes, he thought. If he could cram one into the hole on the front of the safe, he figured he could haul it out.

The other end of the rope would attach to the hitch on the car. Once the thing was out of the water, they would use a dolly to wheel it up into the back of the car. Once there, they would drive outside of the city and find a secluded spot. This was as far as Jake planned out. A relatively simple heist for a potentially massive payout, Jake thought.

The task of opening the safe, he left to Sam. Samantha's father was a well-known artist who specialized in creating metal sculptures out of rusted scraps he picked up from the junkyard. While living at home during college, Sam earned her keep by helping her dad with some of his pieces. She was completely comfortable working with a blowtorch to cut through metal and was convinced she could crack any safe with a sharp enough flame. With her parents out of town this weekend, she dropped by their house to borrow her father's torch and tanks.

Samantha put the keys in the ignition and before starting the car, she turned to Jake and smiled. She didn't remember the last time she felt this excited or nervous, or alive. This giddy feeling reminded her of when she and Jake used to sneak into the back of movie theatres when they were in college. The risk of getting caught stealing a safe from the river only amplified the thrill of sneaking around together. She liked this feeling.

Jake smiled back, and the engine roared to life.

It was a two-minute drive to the site. The streetlights bathed the empty laneways in an orange wash, as if the neighbourhood was seen through a rarely used Instagram filter – too harsh to ever be chosen intentionally.

Samantha stopped the car and the pair looked around before stepping out. The world was quiet and the coast was clear. Being careful not to slam the door behind him, Jake got out and carried the duffel bag to the water. He found the small stick poking out from the mud, just as he'd left it, and he placed his left foot in front of it. The sandals were staying on this time, he thought. He didn't want to have to go looking for them if he needed to get out of there in a hurry.

Counting his paces out quietly, he reached the number eight and plunged his arms into the water. When his fingers hit the muddy bottom, he felt a sharp sense of panic. Did someone get to it before him? He scanned the banks of the river to make sure he wasn't being watched but couldn't see much in the dim light of the crescent moon. Refocusing on the safe, Jake shuffled his feet and felt his way along the bottom for the box, or the pit from where it had been pulled out. It didn't take long for him to find it. The bruised toes on his right foot, now protected by the sandal, made the discovery again. Reaching into the duffel bag strapped tightly against his back, he pulled out a camming device and worked it into the hole on the face of the safe. To his surprise, the first one he chose fit. After giving it a couple of pulls to ensure it would stay, he attached the rope under the water.

Lengths of rope leaked out from the bag as Jake walked towards the shore and out to the trail. After making sure the coast was still clear, he emerged from the trees, drawing a straight line from the safe to the street. Any bends in the rope would put a lot of strain on the line once the car pulled it tight, he thought. Rubbing the rope against the trunks of trees would snap branches or potentially even break the rope. The quieter they could be, the better.

Signalling Samantha to start the car and moving to his location against the curb, Jake thought about the main characters in *Ocean's Eleven* or *The Italian Job*, or even in *Mission Impossible* movies. Those guys had so much more to deal with, he thought. He and Sam didn't have to worry about laser security systems, pressure-sensitive floor panels or the threat of armed guards. They just needed to avoid getting caught by the local bar crowd stumbling home from downtown. If anyone spotted them with the safe, word would travel fast, Jake thought. They would have to live the rest of their lives looking over their shoulders, waiting for an unmarked van to pull up and force them inside.

Looping the rope around the hitch and grabbing the dolly from the trunk, Jake gave a thumbs-up signal to Samantha. She put the car in gear, crept forward until the line tightened and stretched. When the vehicle stopped under the tension in the rope, Jake grit his teeth. The stressed look on his face mirrored the tension on the line. It wasn't until he heard the scrape of metal against rocks that he finally exhaled and waved to Samantha to back up a bit and kill the engine.

Jake unhitched the rope and wrapped it in loose coils as he walked back to the river. The trail was still free of people and no lights came on in nearby houses. We're still good, Jake thought to himself.

As he approached the metal box at the edge of the water, Jake was beside himself with excitement and fear. The faint moonlight bounced off the top of what was clearly a small safe, revealing minor scuffs and scratches. The dial on the front of it was intact, but the hole Jake used to attach the rope, made him curious. Again, dipping into his knowledge of heist movies, Jake recognized there was no handle on the door of the safe. That must be what the hole was from, he thought.

Sitting in mud, it wasn't difficult to slip the dolly under the heavy box. Using the rope to pull against the front of the safe, he leaned his treasure back against the dolly, groaning under the weight. He muscled his way through the mud and across the trail, once again looking to make sure no one was around. When he got to the car, Samantha had already set up a wooden plank to wheel the dolly up. With Sam pushing and Jake pulling, the team heaved the waterlogged treasure into the back of the car and started the engine. Though they sat silent on the short drive home, the look on their faces screamed of joy, disbelief and accomplishment.

* * * * *

They drove out from the city, both trying to keep their emotions in check. The intoxicating feeling of excitement was balanced out by the sobering fear that somehow they'd been caught in the act.

After twenty minutes of driving past fields of soy beans and corn, Samantha pulled off the road down an overgrown dirt path that led into a forested area. The nearest house (according to Google Earth) looked to be nearly a kilometre away and the pair hadn't seen another car since they'd left the city. They were alone.

They wheeled the safe down the wooden plank and sat it on the ground beside the car, face up. They were so focused on recovering the treasure inside the case, they barely paid attention to the stars above them, shining more brilliantly than could ever be seen in the city. Using the flashlight on her phone, Samantha took note of where the latch on door came across to seal the box closed – this is where she would make her cut.

The bright flame kicked on with a steady roar and illuminated the trees around them. As the sparks flew onto the dirt, Jake used the extra light to survey their surroundings, hoping it wouldn't take Sam long to break it open.

After what seemed like an hour, Samantha shut the tank off and set the torch aside. Removing her visor, she stared down at the glowing jagged edge and watched it fade to black. Jake and Samantha stood on either side of the safe and briefly looked at each other before reaching down to uncover their prize. With the rope still attached to the face of the safe, both took hold and gave it a tug. The hinges were sticky with grit and it took both of them a couple of good yanks to get the door open wide enough to see anything. The darkness in the safe was too thick for starlight to reveal any of its contents, but the pair could hear water sloshing around inside.

Samantha juggled her phone to find the flashlight. Once on, the beam was aimed toward the centre of the box, which was half-full of water. The silt, kicked up in their effort to open the door, made the water cloudy and impossible to see through. With heads side-by-side, unblinkingly staring into the brown abyss, Jake's hand found Samantha's and gripped it tightly as they waited patiently for the dust to settle.

* * * * *

They stood there for a minute, staring deep into the clumsy metal box. As the water cleared, they could feel their heightened anxiety quickly fading to exhaustion. Making their way to the ground, the couple lay on their backs, fingers still woven together, and stared up into the sky. With their heads nearly touching and the open safe resting between them, they let out deep sighs and took notice of the stars through a break in the canopy directly above them.

It was a warm summer night and neither of them could remember the last time they stayed up to watch the sunrise together. Exchanging glances without speaking, they decided that this would be how they would spend the morning. For the next two hours, they lay there and listened to the sounds of the night: the wind moving through the trees, the songs of birds ushering in the dawn, and the occasional splashing sound of a pair of crayfish, swimming laps around the inside of the empty safe.

Chris Seto is a multimedia journalist with irons in every fire he can reach. He did his undergraduate degree in New Brunswick, completed journalism school in Ottawa and spent five incredible years with the *Guelph Mercury*, writing stories, taking photos and shooting videos. When the Merc closed, he spent most of 2016 working as a reporter/editor at CBC Hamilton. He's since moved back to Guelph and is currently writing for the *Guelph Mercury Tribune*. Find him online at chrisseto.ca or on Twitter @topherseto.

The Memory Game

Nicole Baute

Clive leaned on the divider that separated his cubicle from Simone's, holding a Trivial Pursuit card. "Okay," he said. "Who was 'Caroline' in Neil Diamond's song Sweet Caroline?"

"That's easy," Simone said. "Caroline Kennedy."

"Right again! Okay, when and where was the longest official tennis match ever played?"

Simone kept her hand on her mouse, showing, she hoped, her reluctance to engage. "Wimbledon, 2010."

Clive frowned. "It says the 2004 French Open."

"You have an old deck," said Simone. "I really should get back to work."

Clive held up the box of cards, shook it and grinned. "Sure, but these will be right here on my desk," he said.

So this was why Simone didn't go out. It wouldn't be like this if she'd skipped Tina Myers's Christmas party again this year, but Susie Wong from payroll had begged her to come along and Susie had always been nice to her. Simone showed up late, wearing what she usually wore to work – black dress pants and a button-up blouse – and everyone else was in Christmas sweaters and sequins, playing an animated game of Charades in the living room. Simone watched from a folding chair against the wall, smiling as she downed three glasses of wine. When Jim Finn stubbed his toe on the coffee table so hard it bled through his sock, everyone decided, woah, maybe this game of Charades is a little too wild, maybe we should all sit down and play Trivial Pursuit instead. And against her best judgement, Simone decided to join in, because she was tired of being a wallflower.

The party ended awkwardly. Mia Campbell threw up in the bathroom. Susie passed out on Jim's shoulder. Everyone else was awake and silent, watching Clive, wearing one of his trademark Hawaiian shirts, lob questions to Simone, who answered every one correctly. Her face was flushed and her palms were sweaty but the adrenaline was strangely refreshing. Until then, she'd done such a good job of convincing everyone she was unremarkable that she'd started believing it herself. But perhaps because of that, or because of the wine, she'd started showing off. They stopped at forty-nine questions. Joe Pacana asked for her autograph. Mika Gordon said she should go on *Jeopardy*!

At the door Tina threw her arms around Simone, squeezing her tight. "I'm so glad you came, Kathy," she said.

Oh yeah, and they thought her name was Kathy.

* * * * *

For reasons she will never understand, Simone remembers everything since February 15, 1990, forty-three days before her fourteenth birthday. It was a Wednesday and it snowed. It was the day Chris Morris gave Meredith Simpson a red rose in the cafeteria in front of everyone. The week before, blushing like a nectarine, splotchy and sweet, Chris had told Simone her dolphin bracelet was "cute," and Simone fell deeply, irrevocably in love. But the roses made it clear that Chris loved Meredith Simpson. Simone spent the rest of lunch feeling sorry for herself at a corner table with pimply Gerald McDonald. After school that same day her father was supposed to pick her up for dinner but didn't because the roads were icy – unusual for Vancouver – which was one of thirty-one excuses he gave her over the course of her adolescence. On the way home she slipped and fell on the sidewalk. Two boys laughed. A black woman in a red coat helped her up and said, "Honey, that is going to leave a bruise." The bruise was in the shape of a horse's head and Simone could not understand why.

Simone remembers her mother telling Dr. Richards that "there is something wrong with her, some kind of mental retardation that makes her remember everything." This was April 26, 1991. Dr. Richards had not flinched at the word retardation, he just pushed his glasses up on his pelican nose and said, "Is that so?" and looked down at Simone was if she were a fascinating organism indeed.

She remembers every physical, every MRI, the word-association games, the tests, that time they tried to hypnotize her, the prescriptions for anxiety, obsessive-compulsive disorder, migraines. The panels of scientists asking her questions and their giant, alien heads. She remembers the first talk show her mother made her go on and how the host accused her of cheating by keeping a journal, and then, in a complete 180, told his two million viewers that she was "an amazing, gifted young woman." She also remembers the last television interview she gave, on November 11, 1996, alongside the memory specialist Dr. Victor Angus, who told the world, "Simone is trapped in a movie of her own life – with all the good parts, and all the bad," and how the rush of sympathetic letters and too-affectionate neighbours made her feel like more of a freak than ever before.

She remembers every time she upset someone and also every time someone upset her. She remembers what she had for breakfast, lunch and dinner on, say, July 3, 2001, or September 22, 2008. She remembers every episode of every sitcom she has ever seen as well as what, if any, significant cultural or political events coincided with them.

She remembers every peal of laughter and what caused it. The same with every tear.

* * * * *

At 5:02, Simone shut down her computer and said a quick goodnight to Clive. She retrieved her winter coat from the coat rack, a relatively new rack that replaced the one that collapsed on April 5, 2011 under the weight of too many umbrellas. She covered her short hair – she used a dark brown dye to cover premature streaks of gre –
—with a crocheted black toque.

She always walked to and from work, even when it was cold and even though it took thirty minutes each way. No matter which route she took, memories found her: the clown who tried to give her a wilted carnation at the corner of Yonge and Richmond, on May 8, 2009, for

example, or the high school classmate she spotted coming out of the
Mercatto, on September 6, 2010. She always avoided Queen Street
East around Empire. That's where she saw an old lady get hit by a
streetcar on July 18, 2011, but if she so much as thought about the fact
that she was avoiding the spot the memory rushed in just the same: the
blood, the low, dull wail. That day Simone was wearing new shoes
and they gave her blisters.

When she got home from work there was a package leaning up
against the door of her apartment. It was smaller than a shoe box and
light, as if filled with only tissue paper. When Simone saw the return
address, her stomach dropped. Sault Ste. Marie. She only knew one
person living there.

As if someone dropped a projector before her eyes, Simone saw
George. He was sitting beside her at the Nutcracker, wriggling his eye-
brows in a bow tie. It was their first night together and they were dis-
cussing his spider tattoo between the sheets. Then they were picking
out a Christmas tree. Eating banana pancakes on the balcony. Dancing
in the living room to You Send Me.

They were driving home from Montreal without speaking.

He was flirting with a redhead in a polka dot dress. He was saying
her inability to take chances on people drove him crazy. But she had
taken a chance on him, hadn't she? And what good had that done? He
was rubbing his face with his hands. Stuffing his clothes into a hockey
bag.

Simone's head pounded. Inside her apartment, she opened the
door to the hallway closet and tossed the box inside. How did he get
her new address? Naturally, she had moved. She'd needed bare walls,
uninhabited rooms. She'd gotten rid of every household item they'd
acquired together, too, although she still remembered them all.

Simone breathed in and out deeply, counting backwards from ten.
When she got to one, she would begin her evening routine. Three...
two...one.

It was a Wednesday, which meant chicken, broccoli and a small
baked potato. She preferred instant mashed, but they reminded her of
her mother, whom she had not spoken to since March 7, 2004. Simone
settled into her La-Z-Boy in front of the television with the TV tray
on her lap and a single square of paper towel. She always started with

the six o'clock news, then *Entertainment Tonight*, then sitcom reruns even though she knew all the punch lines.

She was savouring the last bite of chicken when the telephone rang. She didn't recognize the number. Probably a telemarketer, she thought, prepared to be polite but firm.

"Ms. Trivia!" said the voice on the other end. "I have a good one, I think it might stump you."

"Clive?"

"Yeah, it's me! I hope you don't mind, I got your number from the receptionist. Okay, so, what was Captain Kirk's middle name?"

Simone closed her eyes. "Tiberius," she said.

"Goddamn," said Clive. "Seriously. You're amazing. You're faster than Google! You really should consider going on *Jeopardy*!"

"I'll think about it," she said, looking down at her almost-empty plate.

"Amazing. So, tell me, what's your secret?"

"Dark leafy greens," she told him. She stabbed her fork into the last piece of broccoli.

The next day at work Simone's boss called her into his office. Martin was a small, pale man who often asked questions not because he needed to know the answers, but because he enjoyed watching people squirm.

She chose the blue chair opposite his desk and sat with her legs crossed at the ankles. He leaned forward with his elbows on the table, his lips resting against threaded fingers.

"You wanted to see me?" Simone said, forcing the conversation to begin so it could end.

"Mmm," said Martin. He unthreaded his fingers. "How are you, Kathy?"

"I'm fine, thanks."

"Hmm," he said. "Indeed."

Simone looked at the poster on the wall behind him, a photograph of Mount Everest with the words "Above and Beyond" in a thin serif font, all caps. She looked back at Martin.

"Tell me," he said, leaning forward. "Where do you see yourself in five years?"

"I'm not sure," Simone said. And then, because she didn't want to seem lacking ambition, she added, "I was thinking I'd like to take on another client or two."

Martin grinned. "Kathy," he said. "You are far too modest. What about a little more responsibility? What about a new opportunity?"

"What kind of opportunity?" She didn't know what to do with her hands.

"Well, you tell me. What, would you say, are your strengths? What thing comes most naturally to you?"

She liked systems. She kept her email inbox impeccable.

"I'm very efficient," she said.

"Efficient! Oh, yes, sure you are. But I...well I've heard something about you, Kathy, and I find it interesting. Very interesting. And I can't help but think about what a tremendous asset you could be to this company, frankly, if you are willing to step up. Just think of what we could do with a person of your unique abilities..." Although he continued speaking, Simone only heard keywords, distracted as she was by the memory hurdling towards her. "...human database...gaps in system..."

The hardest part about leaving Vancouver had been saying good-bye to her mother's dog, a little fluffy thing who liked Simone better than anyone. She'd stopped by the house when her mother was at work, selling perfume at the Bay. Trixie was an emotionally percep-tive dog, and after staring with her head cocked at Simone kneeling on the peach hallway carpet, she ran towards her, climbing up to lick her tears. Her breath was terrible, fish and sawdust. It was October 24, 2003.

"...strategic role...secret weapon..." Martin was poking his desk-top aggressively, his eyes lit up like a circus ringmaster's. "Just re-markable..."

She would not miss her mother, not like that. When she got to Toronto she sent her an email saying not to worry, that she was okay. Explaining in as few words as possible her need to start over, in a place where memories did not spring out at her around every corner. Where she was not a minor celebrity – the woman who remembered every-thing. There was also a brief courtship that hadn't worked out, and she needed to get away from that, too. Granville Island was tarnished. So was Chinatown.

"Kathy?" Martin was waiting for an answer to a question Simone had not quite caught. "So what do you think?"

"I…I need some time to think about it."

He nodded, his face suddenly serious. This was an acceptable answer. "Fantastic," he said. "Well, thank you for stopping in." He stood up to shake her hand for the very first time.

Simone struggled to focus all afternoon. She considered looking for a new job. She wondered how she might like living further east – but Halifax was too small, Montreal too French. She counted backwards from a hundred, but it didn't help. At 4:57 p.m., she could not take it any longer and got up to leave. Clive, who usually worked late to catch up – as he was always falling behind – stood, too. He stretched and winked at her. His Hawaiian shirt was green today, covered in yellow palm tree leaves. The last time he wore this particular shirt was when they had cake for Virginia Sheffield's going-away party, May 20, 2015.

They made small talk in the elevator. "It can't be leafy greens," he said. "I just don't buy it." Simone opened her mouth to express exasperation but Clive held up his hand and smiled. "I'm just teasing," he said. "But I do think it's amazing, to have a gift like that."

They walked outside. The street was covered with a thin layer of fresh snow. "Which way are you going?" he asked.

"East," she said.

Clive grinned. "Me too."

They started walking. Simone couldn't think of anything to say, and was relieved when he began to talk. "Maybe everybody has a talent, it's just a matter of figuring out what it is," he said.

Simone looked over. He was squinting, his brow gathered like a drawstring purse. "I think you're probably right," she said.

"My ex-wife, she was an amazing baker. She made these red velvet cupcakes with cream cheese icing…And my kid, he is so amazing at math, I do not understand it. Me? I don't know what I'm good at yet."

"You're good at your job," Simone offered.

Clive made a face that reminded her of November 14, 2013, when he got written up for some inaccuracies in his accounting. "I get by," he said.

The snow crunched beneath their feet. "I'm sure there's something," Simone said.

They walked in silence, past a couple of kids making out on the sidewalk in backpacks and mittens. A thin woman asked for money, claiming she'd been robbed. Clive fished a few quarters out of his pocket and gave them to her. "Thanks, mister," she said, and counting the change clutched in her palm, ran off to catch the streetcar.

Clive smiled sadly. "I think she was lying," he said. "Oh well."

"You're good with people," Simone pointed out.

"You know, I am," said Clive. "That's true."

They kept walking. Simone thought about how she made a pretty good chicken curry – that was her Friday meal. Tomorrow. She thought about how when she was a kid she wanted to be a zoologist. She'd dressed up as one for Halloween.

She didn't realize they were at Queen and Empire until it was too late.

"Oh," she said.

The shoes had been beige and pinched around the heel. The Band-Aids weren't sticking very well in the heat, and Simone walked slow and awkwardly, thinking about a small mistake she'd made at work. The woman was Chinese, hardscrabble, pulling a small fabric cart filled with bottles. She came out of the park and shuffled across the sidewalk, about hundred metres in front of Simone. Simone looked right to see a group of teenage boys playing basketball. One was shouting, "Brian! Bri! Over here!" Something compelled her to look left. She turned her head just in time to catch the woman step out from behind a parked car and into the streetcar's path. The driver's horrified face. The sound of screeching metal; the thud. How Simone had opened her mouth to scream, "No!" but could not be sure that sound came out.

"Are you okay?" It was Clive asking. Simone was on the curb, her head buried in her hands. The memory was a migraine, pounding. The woman wailed, a low, dull sound. Simone knelt by her side with the streetcar driver, a middle-aged man about to cry. People running, bottles rolling across the street. Blood. "Are you okay?" Clive asked again. He was confused, he was searching her face for clues, his breath white against the winter air.

"I'm not sure," Simone finally said.

* * * * *

There are moments Simone turns to when things feel out of control. When counting does not help. Like precious stones, she takes them out and polishes them, lines them up in a row.

The beach, age seventeen, with her cousin Mallory. Simone had just gotten her driver's licence. They drove to a stretch of shore where there wasn't anyone around, just seagulls, stripped down to their underwear and ran to the water. Simone was thin, her white cotton bra covered in tiny blue stars. When they hit the ocean's edge Mallory kept running, water splashing wildly around her thighs, her waist, her chest, and Simone felt compelled to follow even though the water was cold. She winced and laughed and then gave in, letting the water wash over her. The waves were big, cresting at two feet, and Mallory suggested they try body surfing; she'd seen it on TV. And so they attacked each wave, throwing their bodies without fear. They kept going, laughing and laughing, until they were covered in seaweed and snot, their white skin slapped red. "Simone!" Mallory shouted. "We're stronger than the ocean!"

Or, one time her father did show up, and he took her to the aquarium. In the car on the way home he thought she was sleeping and said, "Little girl. I know I'm a jerk sometimes, but I try, and I love you, I do."

* * * * *

When Simone got home from work, she mixed herself a gin and tonic. It wasn't part of the routine, but she needed it. She sat on a barstool with her elbows on the counter and the television off, drinking slowly and listening to the clock tick. When her glass was empty, Simone went to the closet to retrieve George's box.

She was right, it was filled mostly with tissue paper. Purple, and she could tell from all the creases it had been reused. She pulled the paper out and set it on the counter.

In the bottom of the box was a dreamcatcher. One of those thinga-mabobs made of fine wire and suede and feathers you aren't supposed to call tacky. Simone knew what they were but had no specific mem-ory of them, which was surprising. She frowned, holding it up to the light. She felt nothing until she noticed a little piece of white paper that had fallen out. It was in George's scribbly cursive.

Saw this and thought of you. – G

Simone was mildly annoyed, but she hung the dreamcatcher in her window anyway. Then she sat down in her La-Z-Boy, even though she hadn't made dinner yet, and reached for the remote control. On CTV, her friend Marcia MacMillan was telling her about a new study that found traces of dangerous plastic in breast milk, but Simone wasn't paying attention. When she heard the phone ring, she wondered how long it had been ringing for.

It was Clive, she knew the number this time. She hesitated, then answered.

"Are you okay?" he asked.

"Yeah," she said. "Thanks."

There was an awkward silence.

"Sometimes," she said slowly, "I have flashbacks. They can be very powerful. I saw an accident at that spot once, and it comes back every time I pass it."

"I thought it was something like that," Clive said.

"You did?"

"Yeah," Clive said. "And I was thinking, maybe you need to make a new memory."

"What?"

"Like, a better one – a better memory – at that spot, to cover up the bad one." Clive paused and Simone said nothing. "When my wife left, I didn't want to do anything, go anywhere," Clive continued. "But then I thought, I owed it to Evan, so we started going around to all our old haunts, just the two of us. Covering 'em up. I took him to our favourite pub and we shared French fries. We played Frisbee in the park in front of the OCAD building where we once...well, never mind. It helped."

Simone did not know what to say to that. She'd muted the television set. She could hear the clock tick.

"I'm getting a promotion," she told Clive.

"Well, hey! We should celebrate. Dinner, tomorrow?"

Simone shifted in her chair and looked at the dreamcatcher in the closed window. If it were open, she imagined, the feathers would move.

"You still there?" Clive asked.

"I'm here," Simone said. She couldn't remember the last time she'd been on a proper date. How was that possible?

"Dinner would be nice," Simone said.

Nicole Baute was a summer reporter with the *Mercury* in 2007 and went on to be a staff reporter with *The Toronto Star*. She now works as a writing strategist and editor for small business owners, helping them grow their businesses through website copy, blog posts, ebooks and more. Semi-nomadic, she's lived in Ottawa, Toronto, Vancouver, Accra (Ghana) and New Delhi (India).

Nicole's short stories have been published in *Joyland* and the *Feathertale Review*, and in 2013 she co-edited an anthology of women's writing called *EAT IT*, a lively romp through the curious place where gender and food coalesce. She holds an undergraduate degree in English, a master's degree in journalism, and a certificate in creative writing. Passionate about the power of self-expression, Nicole teaches writing in the online school Story is a State of Mind and through her own website, www.nicolebaute.com.

Strokin' the Stash:

The Bubble People's Pursuit of the Moustached Class

Rob O'Flanagan

"Strokin' the Stash." It was a popular saying in the 1970s, reflecting a general optimism and sense of fun and frivolity. Although there was nothing frivolous about stroking the stash, based as it was on the deeply held beliefs of the time.

Television ad campaigns, household colour schemes, elaborate cloud-seeding operations, various forms of the arts, including motion pictures, opera, and limited-edition t-shirts, all dedicated to, and issuing forth from, the belief and practice of strokin' the stash.

If you could stroke the moustache of one of the deities of popular culture, there was a strong belief that the tips of the fingers through which you stroked the follicles would act as a lightning rod, through which the powers of the universe would course, imparting good fortune and fame on the stroker, along with a growing list of powers. Rain maker, touch healer, small animal magnet, sex guru, seer of things unseen, attractor of general good fortune.

Due to various salves and serums, implants, injections, invocations and glues, women, too, grew moustaches in those days, though never sideburns. And so, the famous, the elevated, the worshipped of both genders wore moustaches. The bushier the better. And it was such an interesting decade for this reason, as well as for several other reasons which are, in relative terms, extraneous.

"Strokin' the stash." It was a reflection of the philosophical underpinnings of a marvelous and optimistic decade in which people –

at least those that could afford the $1,400 – floated around in clear la-tex bubbles that had a clever system of propellers of various sizes that steered the single occupant through specially designed corridors. The infrastructure expenditures alone were astronomical. The corridors had been more or less bubble-proofed – no sharp corners, no protrud-ing antenna or barbwire, no clotheslines, or prickly balcony railings, or children playing with darts or other projectiles.

The moustached class had their own means of transportation which involved a most elaborate system of robotic hummingbirds attached to the clothing at various locations. And, of course, there was a very sanitary pneumatic tube system for indoor travel, so that they never really had to the touch the ground. Their mode of transport was very appropriate to their station.

There were other wildly original innovations in that wonderful time, like hallucinogenic sunglasses that re-proportioned everything, so that you could step over or walk under a skyscraper, or, for that matter, ride the back of a cat or a squirrel and take some of the load off of your tired feet. Those without bubbles, those with no access to pneumatics or robotic hummingbirds, they had to cover great dis-tances on foot and appreciated at least the illusion of foreshortened travel.

And, there was the fabulous ReVoice, a small mechanical box, about the size of a tin container of Aspirin that you wore on a choker under your turtleneck sweater. When activated, this marvel allowed you to speak in an assortment of voices and tongues – chimpanzee or Mahatma Gandhi, various song birds, stars of yesteryear, stage and screen. So many practical and fun uses. Everybody wanted one. Like the hallucinogenic sunglasses, the ReVoice did not come cheap.

The floating bubble people were trying to rise, trying to get ahead in life. That was apparent to all. Even the moustached class, members of which were above everything, nevertheless appreciated the bub-ble people for their ambition, and devotion. They were given spe-cial concessions, and often wore the ReVoice. They did so especially when floating to the upper storeys and the fabled roof-top gatherings, very upper crust, where they hoped to be engaging conversationalists among the in-crowd, which included, most often – but not always, one or two of the moustached – the magical, the magnificent moustached.

And of course you, the "bubbler," the "floater," the "riser," would find some excuse to veer your bubble towards them, find some way, any way, to get within stroking distance, which was necessarily very close.

Back in the 1970s, people would do just about anything to be famous, to have powers, to have status, because these attributes, these higher qualities meant you truly existed. It meant you had arrived, you were fulfilled, you belonged. It meant you had heart, you had what it took, you had that special thing that made you special, and so, so dearly loved but all.

Sadly, that marvelous decade – so elevated, so feverish – was unsustainable. In hindsight, it was so predictable. But in the midst of it there was no way to conceive that it would end, and end abruptly, and for reasons that seemed so small, so pragmatic, so fickle and human.

Too many demands on one's energy. Too many crushing disappointments. Too many bubbles burst. How many countless thousands came so close, within a facial hair's width of strokin' the stash, only to be shoved aside, blown off course by a sneeze or a sudden gust of wind, never to get so close again.

Finally, some – in groups like the Babies Bottoms and the Ordinariaires – when the end was nigh, became emboldened enough to decry the chase of moustached. They plastered the bubble corridors with posters with clever sayings like, "Look! Look how fat the floaters grow!" Or, "Burst the bubble and make some trouble."

Eventually, the side-effects of wearing hallucinogenic sunglasses became all too apparent. Habituated wearers couldn't tell a cat from a fire hydrant, or a cottage from a suspension bridge. They lost touch with reality.

And the chronic ReVoicers, they all began to sound the same – thousands of the Gandhi-voiced congregating in parks and along riverbanks, saying the same things in exactly the same way. Hundreds of sound-alike James Cagneys or Greta Garbos milling about the record stores and second-hand clothing shops.

It all grew so very, very unoriginal. And in that great decade, no one could tolerate the accusation of unoriginality, the sickening possibility of it.

And so, there was a turning against the moustached class, and a concurrent decline in bubble sales. People began to ask if it was not simply better to walk than to float, better to speak with one's own voice than to speak in the voice of Humphrey Bogart, or a blue whale. And a critical mass ultimately agreed that, yes it would be better. Yes, it would.

And strokin' the stash went into steep decline. It fell into disrepute, until it was relegated to small pockets, outposts, compounds, encampments, where moustaches grew obscenely bushy and bubbles collected moss and mold. And, it was not unusual in these places to find devotees wearing three or four pairs of overlapping hallucinogenic sunglasses, or two, three ReVoice – pawing the air in front of their faces as though everything was a moustache.

———————————

Rob O'Flanagan began working as a journalist at the *Mercury* in early 2007, moving to Guelph from Sudbury, where he had spent about twelve years at the *Sudbury Star*. He felt immediately at home at the *Merc* despite being far less intelligent than most, if not all of the newsroom staff at the time, and it was a large staff. But the bawdy and dark humour, and the incredibly open-minded, creative and fun culture made it a great fit for him. He started to come into his own as a journalist in that environment. While Rob does not have good recall when it comes to his past work – it is all a blur - he counts his three weeks in South Africa and Lesotho with a delegation from Bracelet of Hope in 2009 as his most memorable and most personally transformative assignment. He has not seen the world quite the same since. His most difficult writing assignment was being asked to pen the *Mercury*'s final feature/obituary story. He doubled over in grief after completing it. Shortly after the *Mercury* came to an end, Rob went web-side, putting his writing, reporting and photography skills, and his knowledge and love of Guelph, to work for Village Media's *GuelphToday*.com.

The Pager

Brian Whitwham

Once the little red lights flicker, she will be dead.

In the meantime, there was a lot to do: bags to pack in the car, people to call and arrangements to make. He would soon be making funeral arrangements, picking a charity for donations, shutting down his mother's bills, collecting her banking information and sorting through her tax records. But for now, he was fastened to a bench in the hospital lobby, in blue jeans and a t-shirt, too unsure of himself to move. Here he was: thirty years old and about to lose his mother. He was slumped forward, his chest seemed heavy and he felt helpless.

There was a small, black, triangular disk in his hands: a device with a collection of round red lights on its perimeter. A nurse had given him it as he walked out of the intensive care unit. She said they would use it to "page" him if "anything happened".

He knew what this meant because any hope for good news had been eliminated. Once the pager lights up and the disc vibrates, everything is over. In the meantime, he wasn't supposed to be wasting time on a bench in the lobby. He was supposed to be at his mother's side. He figured that he should feel sad, afraid, or at least able to move. Instead, he felt detached, numb and disoriented.

The last few hours had felt like a week and he kept replaying them over in his head.

"It could happen at any minute but she won't survive the afternoon," the physician had told him. "At this point, we should just let nature to take its course."

The physician, a woman with green eyes and short, salt and pepper hair, had come across as a very caring and empathetic doctor. He figured she had given this speech hundreds of times. She was a specialist in internal medicine and her reassurances sounded logical, clinical; even warm.

But this didn't make the process any easier.

The man had dropped everything and rushed to the hospital that morning from another city. The staff had told him he needed to get there as soon as possible to authorize an emergency surgical procedure on his mother. The drive usually took more than three hours but he had made it that day in less than two and a half. By the time he arrived at his mother's room, she wasn't there. A young nurse with red hair explained that his mother had been moved to the intensive care unit. They no longer needed him to sign anything. The nurse had beckoned the man to a private office. In a gentle voice, she asked him to sit down and wait for the attending physician. He knew by then that something was wrong. Despite her kind demeanour, the nurse refused to provide any direct answers to his questions. She simply said that he would need to speak to the doctor.

The discussion with the physician had seemed to unfold in a haze. As he sat on the bench, the man could only vividly recall one phrase that kept running through his mind, "We should just let nature take its course."

He had stood at his mother's side in the intensive care unit after accepting the doctor's recommendation for end-of-life treatment. His mother lay in the hospital bed. Her eyes were closed and she was silent, except for a mild snore that tracked her breathing. There were no plans for surgery and his mother likely wasn't going to survive the afternoon. There was an oxygen mask on her face and a confusing array of tubes and wires connected to her body. The doctor had assured him that the hospital staff would provide enough pain medication to virtually eliminate his mother's discomfort. "How would they even what kind of pain she was in?" he thought.

Although his mother seemed peaceful, the monitors surrounding her bed graphically displayed her body's resistance to its predicament. Her blood pressure had dropped. Her breathing was laboured. Her head made sharp, twitching movements every few minutes and her feet did the same. Her heartbeat kept increasing and decreasing in speed, seemingly defiant to the cascading failure of other organs throughout her body. It was clear that her body was at war with itself, and she didn't know that the result had already been fixed.

But it was the touch of his mother's hands that troubled the man more than anything else. Although they were as smooth and slight as they had always been, the warmth that the man was accustomed to was gone. His mother's circulation had slowed and her fingers were like ice. The man had repeatedly tried to cover her hands with blankets in an effort to keep them warm. Even before the third nurse gave him the same sad, sympathetic glance as the previous two, he realized that his efforts were hopeless.

This had nearly broken him. The chill in his mother's hands, the jarring sounds from the monitors, and the gentle but hopeless expressions from the nursing staff had driven home that this was happening today. That's why the man had left the ICU. The months spent trying to come to grips with her grim diagnosis – and the additional months spent in the constant cycle of faint hope, followed by treatment and more bad news – had not prepared him for this afternoon in the ICU.

He had grabbed his mother's purse, her glasses, and a flower arrangement from a nearby table that had been left for her the previous week. He had gone to the parking lot to load everything into his car. He had been on his way back up to the ICU when he stopped at the bench.

He was unsure of how long he had been sitting there but the lights hadn't flickered. He wondered whether the pager might be broken.

He had always found hospitals to be strange places. Lives were beginning and ending every day within these walls, and on this afternoon, he felt acutely aware of his surroundings. There was an older man outside the front entrance with wispy grey hair, an oxygen tank at his side, and a cigarette in his mouth. There was a middle-aged woman pushing a wheelchair in the direction of the hospital's cafeteria. She was speaking to the teenage boy in the chair who was nodding as he smiled at her. He had a Detroit Tigers hat on his head and a cast on his left leg. The man figured the boy had to be the woman's son. Across the lobby, there was a younger couple who were holding hands as they slowly made their way through the rotating glass door at the exit. The man was carrying a car seat with an infant who was probably only a few days old.

In the centre of a large atrium near an elevator bay, there was a security guard speaking to a thin woman with red hair and freckled skin at the information booth. Both were laughing and they seemed oblivious to the gravity of the circumstances unfolding in every corridor of the building.

All of these unique situations and interactions around him were a welcome distraction to what was happening in the ICU. At one point, the man was even able to muster the strength and will to lift himself from the bench. He stood up and took a couple of steps towards the elevator bay. But he then – almost automatically – circled around and sat back down. The black triangular disc in his hands was still dark. The red lights hadn't flickered. The object was as lifeless as he felt.

"People aren't supposed to buckle like this," the man thought. "These are supposed to be the moments in which we stand up."

But he had never considered himself a particularly strong person. He had thrown up before taking his driver's test at sixteen years old. His mother had pretended not to know.

He used to cry before swimming lessons when he was a child. But it was his mother's encouraging glance that had prompted him to jump from the high board in the deep end at nine years old, and then competitively in races as a teenager.

The last time the man felt like this, he had lost his father in similar circumstances. With his father, it had been a lengthy battle with cancer so there had been more time for everyone to prepare. He could remember pleading with his mother, at nine years old, when his father was in the final stages of the disease. At all costs, he wanted to avoid having to go into the room at the hospice to say "goodbye".

"What's the point?" he had asked his mother. "Dad won't hear us anyway." As always, his mother had seen through this act. Though she knew he was afraid, she was careful not to belittle him. This had been one of her greatest skills. In those kinds of moments, there was something about the confident and reassuring manner in which she extended her hand that made it impossible to argue. The only response that made sense was to take his mother's hand and follow her. "I'm here," she would say.

His mother had always been his rock and now, she was sinking. As he sat on the bench, the man realized she would no longer be there to reassure him, keep him level or simply tell him, "I'm here." He was staring at the ground, lost in uncertainty about how he would manage without her. He had been so consumed in his own thoughts that he hadn't noticed anyone else approach the bench.

"Daddy?"

When he raised his head, the man's glance met squarely with two blue eyes staring intently back at his. It was his seven-year-old daughter. Her mother had dropped her at the hospital entrance while she went to find a parking spot. It was clear the little girl had been crying. The paths travelled by tears were still visible on her cheeks. She stood in a purple coat with her arms hanging at her sides. Her blonde hair had been wound into a tight pony tail and she was clutching a bright pink piece of paper in her left hand. It was a card that her grandmother would never read. The man wrapped his arms around her. The little girl was silent but she buried her face into the man's shoulder and from the vibration of her body, he knew she was crying.

After a few seconds, she backed away and wiped her eyes. "I don't want to go in by myself," she said.

At that moment, the man's back straightened. He leaned forward and pulled himself to his feet. Something about his daughter's voice and her words made everything clear.

The feelings of fear and confusion that had pinned him to the bench before his daughter's arrival weren't gone. They just didn't matter as much anymore. The urge to protect his daughter in that moment now seemed every bit as reassuring as his mother's encouragement when he was a boy. The man wondered whether his mother had felt this way when his father died.

He looked down at the little girl for a moment. She looked up and held his stare. His expression was serious – but reassuring – and after a few seconds, he extended his hand.

"I'm here," he said.

The little girl took his hand and they walked towards an elevator in silence.

"What's that?" she said, pointing to the black triangle in her father's other hand.

The pager device remained dark and motionless. The man knew they would be back in the ICU before the lights flickered.

"It's nothing," he said.

Brian Whitwham worked at the *Guelph Mercury* from 2004 until 2007. He covered stories throughout Guelph and Wellington County in a variety of beats, including crime, health, business, education, sports and politics. In 2007, he became the newspaper's city hall report until he left the media business for law school. He also spent time as a reporter at the *London Free Press* and *The Record*, in Kitchener. Brian now works as a lawyer, in London, where he lives with his wife Lauren and their two children, Emily and Michael.

A Comeback Attempt

Brian Williams

"Reach in the back and grab me a cold one, would ya?"

The request came from Norm, who was setting the usual fine example for his boy, Hank, on the five-hour drive south from their hometown to Guelph. Hank was going to play junior hockey for the Storm. The top draft pick a few months earlier, he was just what the hockey gods had ordered. He was big, fast and knew how to put the puck in the net.

Norm was never much of a hockey player himself. He lacked the expected story about injuries that stopped him from going pro. But years of watching a lot of games on TV, typically well-oiled on beer, harder booze, or a mix of both, convinced him he was quite the expert on the game. It as ever-eager to advise his boy on the mistakes he had made during games. Yes, it was Norm's coaching that led Hank to this day. Just ask Norm, he would tell you.

With about twenty minutes remaining in the drive, Hank popped open another can of beer for his dad. "Cans are better for driving," Norm always said. "Easier to hold between your legs, cops think it's pop if they get a quick glance. And, the empties rolling around in the back on the floor don't make as much noise as bottles when you take a corner too fast."

It was just one of the many valuable lessons Hank was taking with him into his new life on the path to glory as a pro hockey player. There was little doubt he'd be a pro one day. All the scouts liked what they had seen of him at tournaments during his minor hockey years and it seemed it was just a matter of how much desire Hank had to make the dream come true.

The Storm's general manager was eager to greet Hank. They had met a few times but hadn't seen each other since draft day. He escorted Hank to the main dressing room to introduce him to the veterans he hadn't yet met. He also wanted to show him the stall that already had his name on it.

This training camp wasn't a matter of whether Hank would make the team, it was figuring out how much he'd be able to help it. Still, Hank would leave nothing to chance. He was going to make sure he would not be sent home.

Next, it was time to meet his billet family. Mrs. Duke – "Oh, call me Julia" – was fortyish, with a big smile and a Storm jacket covered in pins and buttons that had all the players' faces on them.

Out in the parking lot, Hank retrieved two suitcases from the trunk while Julia and Norm shared small talk. Hank could hear Julia giving directions to the nearest beer store and he couldn't wait to see Norm driving away – hopefully forever.

"Good luck, boy. Remember everything I taught you."

Hank sighed. "Thanks for the lift."

* * * * *

"Oh, you're still here," she said. "I thought you'd left an hour ago but it looked like your car still out in the parking lot, so I figured I'd come see if everything was alright."

Hank was sitting on the edge of his dad's bed, staring off into space. The voice that had brought him back into the room belonged to Penny, his dad's favourite nurse.

"You OK?" she asked.

Hank hoped she was asking a general question and hadn't seen that he quickly wiped a tear from his cheek before turning toward her.

"Where's your dad?" she threw in, before getting an answer to the first question.

"He's in the bathroom, making his third 'one last pit stop' before hitting the road."

That line got a chuckle out of Penny. Hank told her that every time they started making their way toward the car Norm would see someone else that he just had to tell goodbye. It was odd behaviour for a man who spent most of his life blind to those around him, unless he had something to gain from befriending them.

Yet, through the eyes of Penny, there was nothing odd about it. In the year she had known Norm he had become a fun-loving resident of the retirement community. Funny what not having access to booze had done for his personality.

Had Norm been like that when Hank was a boy, would Hank's life have turned out differently? Would he have been so motivated to make it as a hockey player so he could escape the family home? Would his mother have stayed, instead of reaching her limit and tearfully leaving Hank behind when he was ten?

Thinking about his mother remained the one thing that could make Hank cry and that's what he was doing when Penny walked in.

"Your dad has really been talking a lot about this week away. He's really been working hard on his exercises since the last fall so that he'd be strong enough to go away without requiring any extra help.

"He's told me all about your girls and how much he's looking forward to seeing them."

As they spoke, Norm emerged quietly from the washroom and was standing behind Penny with a big grin on his face.

"Care for one last spin before I go, darlin'"

His voice startled her. Before she could answer, Norm grabbed her hand and held it high so she could twirl underneath as he butchered the melody of some old song. "Dee dee dum, dum dee dee…"

Penny knew changing the subject was her way out. "Are you finally done in that washroom? Your son wants to get on the road before the weather turns bad."

"Ya," Hank added. "We've got a long drive and we don't want to make ourselves late for dinner."

"OK, OK," Norm chimed in. "But you know me, never pass up an opportunity to hit the can before hitting the road. Even if you don.t think you have to go."

"Yes, dad, we're all familiar with your philosophy. Now, can we go?"

* * * * *

It had been a long time since Norm's last trip north. During Hank's three years playing for the Storm, Norm found himself spending more and more time in Guelph. He was able to capitalize on his status as the star player's dad, which meant most of the beer he drank was paid for by others. People mistakenly thought being his friend would give them access to Hank, but that couldn't have been further from the truth. Hank wanted nothing to do with his dad during those days. He had a good thing going and wasn't about to let Norm ruin it.

He preferred to pretend his billeting family was his real family. The Dukes' two teenage boys were like brothers and they liked having a member of the family who was a celebrity. And, when Hank wasn't at the rink or pretending to be a Duke, he could be found with a raven-haired beauty named Sandra.

Sandra and her friends were regulars at the arena, looking to date players who had potential to make it to the National Hockey League. Latching on to the right teenage boy, a couple of years away from having a large bank account, was an inexact science. Hank, however, had been so highly touted before he even got to town it wasn't a matter of whether the girls would target him, it was only a matter of determining which one would get her hands on him. It's unclear whether Sandra or Hank had been the instigator, but she knew the blue-chip prospect was hers ever since the day during that first training camp when she noticed he was fascinated with the pattern stitched on the back pockets of her designer jeans.

So, when Hank did turn pro, Sandra was along for the ride. During his third pro season, he was playing well and it was clear his next contract would be a healthy one. It was the perfect time for her to become pregnant and she did – with the first of their two daughters. After playing for three teams over nine seasons, Hank's knees had taken all of the abuse they would be able to handle so it was time to hang up the skates.

Life without hockey, however, couldn't be imagined. So he turned to coaching. After two years as an assistant in the minor leagues, Sandra's pleas for stability finally had sway. Hank landed the head coaching job with the university team in the hometown he had been so desperate to leave more than a dozen years earlier. His success as a player made him a celebrity star in the north. So, his return generated excitement. Two university championships in his first five years behind the bench gave him job security and Sandra and the girls were happy. That meant he could be happy too.

It was odd, though, him being back up north while Norm continued to live in Guelph. Norm had met a woman named Sheila who enjoyed the drink almost as much as he did. And she had money from a divorce and a nice roof to live under, so there had been no reason for him to leave. After that relationship turned toxic a couple of years ago, Norm tested the waters with the idea of relocating north to be near his only family. Sandra made it quite clear though that he was unwelcome. If he moved back he wouldn't be hanging around.

Her dislike for Norm took root early as Hank told her stories of his dad's drunken ways and how he had driven his mother away. And then Norm sealed the deal at their wedding reception, grabbing the microphone and informing his fellow guests that he "always knew some puck bunny would get her claws into Hank." Norm thought he was funny. He was the only one who did.

* * * * *

Now, here they were making their first long-distance drive together since that day Norm had brought Hank to Guelph for the start of his junior career. Norm had a bad fall about a year ago and needed to move into a care setting. He hated going there. For him it was a place of too many rules.

"This cannot be where I play out my final years. I cannot be in this bloody place until I die," he said, on the day he was obliged to call the place his new home.

Yet, about three months into his time at "the home", as he called it, his attitude improved. He started taking his rehabilitation seriously to get strength back into his left leg, which had been in a cast. And, he was calling Hank a couple of times a week just for the sake of calling. Without booze informing his thought process the two actually started to have nice conversations and build a relationship. A couple of times

Norm floated the idea of visiting but Hank changed the subject and never mentioned it to Sandra.

* * * * *

"I talked to your dad today."

It took Hank a few seconds to process what he had just heard. It sounded a lot like Sandra had just told him she had had a conversation with Norm.

"He called me this afternoon. If I had recognized the phone number I probably wouldn't have answered, and when I heard his voice I considered hanging up. But he said he was calling to apologize for what he said about me at our wedding and it caught me off guard.

"Before I knew it we were talking about the girls and I was agreeing to let him visit for a few days. You're picking him up on Thanksgiving weekend."

The drive north was uneventful – small talk and a couple of stops to use restrooms. Norm seemed most interested in spending time with his granddaughters.

Dinner was beyond ready when they arrived. They got in about ninety minutes later than had been planned. It wasn't the best way to start the weekend with Sandra but she was surprisingly not angry. Very welcoming, actually. Seeing her hug Norm was weird for Hank. The girls were interested to meet their grandpa and the rest of that Saturday night and Sunday and Monday were very pleasant. Strangely so for Hank. Who was this man in his house? It certainly wasn't his dad, at least not the one he grew up with.

Norm had talked about wanting to visit a couple of old friends and made plans to do so on Tuesday. Hank and Sandra had expected him to be back early in the evening but he didn't show up in time to say goodnight to the girls. With no definite itinerary there was no sense in going to look for him. He'd be back when he got there. He knew where a key was hidden. They'd talk in the morning. But the only thing that came on Wednesday morning was a knock on the door. It was a provincial police officer. He had a photo of Norm and asked Hank if he was the son of the man in the picture.

65

On Tuesday, Norm had hired a cab to take him to a liquor store for a bottle of scotch and, then, to the river an hour north of the city where he used to fish. He told the cabbie he was meeting someone but was about half an hour early. It was a nice fall day and the driver didn't question him. Before driving away, the cabbie counted the wad of bills Norm had handed him and watched as Norm sat on the dock and took a swig of scotch.

Norm eventually drank enough courage to steal a canoe from the closed-for-the-season rental place and head out on the water with his bottle. It was unclear how long he spent paddling but he made his way to a waterfall and drowned after crashing into the rocks at the bottom of it. A fit, sober person, one with a will to live could have survived that fall and the plunge into the surrounding, chest-deep waters, but not someone intent on never returning to "the home".

A hiker spotted the overturned canoe late Tuesday afternoon and Norm's body soon after. Hank asked the police officer to show him the spot. From a small bridge overlooking the waterfall, Hank thought about both of his parents. For the first time ever, his tears were for his father.

When Hank returned home he told the girls grandpa had gone back home to Guelph. No more questions were asked about why daddy seemed sad.

Later that evening, after the girls were asleep and Hank made the phone call to Guelph to let Penny know. Then, he decided to gather up the few belongings Norm had left in the guestroom.

Opening Norm's suitcase to put in pyjamas and a pair of pants, he spotted a folded piece of paper with "Hank" written on it. It wasn't a long note apologizing for the bad times and telling him he loved him. The message was short and simple:

"Thanks for the lift."

Brian Williams worked in the *Guelph Mercury* newsroom for about 27 years. After three years as a sports reporter and photographer, he held a series of editing roles, including city editor for his final ten years. He helped lead a team to a National Newspaper Award and was proud each year as he watched colleagues earn Ontario Newspaper Award nominations and victories. Still, one of his proudest moments happened when he was a copy editor on the night desk. He came into work one evening to find notes from an intern and a veteran reporter, both thanking him for his help the night before as they worked on difficult stories under the pressure of deadline. When the newspaper closed he was also the editor of *Guelph Life* magazine and is currently the editor of *Grand* magazine.

The Accountant King

Phil Andrews

I expected so much more. The caller had said the home was "plastered with Elvis stuff."

When I arrived, I saw just thirteen black-and-white photocopies of the same picture of The King. Yellow masking tape moorings held the econo Presley posters into the bare, silver branches of a small maple tree and into those a leafless shrub next to it. Each Presley picture's base bore the same handwritten message, in red marker ink. "Happy 50th birthday Mitch," was Sharpie-tattooed across a hand and part of the chest of the rock legend in each of them.

There had been fifty of the Presley prints on the grounds and exterior of Mitch Grissom's home at one point before the sun was out that morning. That's what the caller to the newsroom had said. But, the January wind had whittled the count. When I parked my car, one of the 'Young Elvis' birthday tributes blew across the snow-padded lawn and swept briefly against the driver's side of my vehicle.

Elvis lived. Momentarily. On the large creased page that slapped against my car's window, he was upside down and holding a boxy microphone to his open mouth. Then, like the real Elvis, he was suddenly gone. I imagined some nearby fence wallpapered with a convention of the Elvis birthday greetings – ushered there from Grissom's property by the upstaging wind. A sharp gust bullied the car's door as I opened it. I wondered whether I had made a mistake in coming.

It had seemed a good tip to the newsroom. It had seemed a story that might dance on the news wires – if it were true, and served up well.

It had felt like a great little story to get noticed over, at this newspaper and beyond it, on my first shift as its weekend reporter.

To take it on meant tacking on an assignment to my shift. It had been made clear to me that one didn't drop an assignment issued here. So, if I jumped on the tip to look in on a purported "Elvis maniac," on the birthday he shared with his idol, I would be working that in amid my mandated stories. I knew I would also be updating the strike at the sawmill, talking to high school students doing a twenty-four hour famine and interviewing people on a local street peeved about damage the city snowplow had recently done to their lawns.

Grissom was an accountant. He failed to give off a maniac vibe when I called him about whether there was anything to the story tip about him. He told me only that he was "a big fan" of Presley's. He confirmed he and Elvis were both January 8 babies. The King would have been sixty on this day. The Accountant was fifty. But the caller said Grissom's house had to be seen for its "Elvis elements" and Grissom said I could head over and see them and have a word with him.

He was waiting for my arrival. He greeted me near his then lightly Elvis-ed tree and bush. He was wearing a blue oxford shirt and a black tie with little White Jumpsuit Elvises all over it. It had been a birthday gift from his wife that day. He had tied it on to be in the photo that I had sold him on taking, of him and his home – before I had come out and taken in the disappointing scene.

The elements for composing a compelling shot were lacking. But, I figured those at hand were likely to be the best to ever be available given the disappearing posters and what I feared would be nothing of greater note or visual appeal inside the house. Grissom grinned a stiff, wedding-day photo shoot smile for me as I unfurled my camera. I captured his face, most of his tie and a portion of two of the remaining birthday posters in a few photos. Then, he invited me into his home to let me interview him.

We sat in a living room that looked never to have been lived in – on a love seat set wrapped in slip covers. Our feet rested on clear, plastic, floor runners over his family's ivory coloured carpet.

Grissom clearly admired Elvis. He said he had "all his albums," had "seen all his movies" and had "been to Graceland."

All his quotes were like that. Flaccid. I wondered if he was holding back but suspected with increasing dread that wasn't so. Maybe I'd just been over-sold over the phone about a purportedly wild and newsworthy local Elvis nut. As Grissom answered my last question, I was not even taking notes of what he said. Instead, I came to stare at a large, framed family photo on a table beside us. He followed my glance and identified his wife and daughter as the two people in the photo with him. His wife was a nurse. His daughter aspired to be one. She looked like her mom. Same eyes. Same thin smile. Same short, dark hair. Almost matching pale blue blouse too.

Silence billowed in the room.

I considered just saying my thank-you, extending a hand for a farewell shake and clearing out. But to salvage this as a story I still needed some telling detail that screamed about how Grissom was a special Elvis fan. So, I complained to Grissom.

I told him I was surprised someone had called the paper about him or even given his front yard "The King treatment" given how controlled his thing for Elvis seemed to be. Grissom remained silent but his neck reddened as I spoke.

When I finished, he blurted: "I'll show you my Elvis room."

He rose, turned and walked away. I followed him out the room, around a corner, through a short hallway and down stairs to his basement door. He opened it and held it wide for me to pass by.

We were no longer in Mitch Grissom, the accountant/husband/father's house. Life-sized, costumed, wax figures of Elvis – from three Elvis-time periods – stood in recessed, spot-lit alcoves, along one wall. Along the back of the room a projector was screening Viva Las Vegas. Grissom pointed out the unit was loaded with video discs of all Presley's movies and set to loop them continuously. Another part of the room featured a wardrobe of Presley-wear. There were the sunglasses, side-burned wigs, even a white jump suit. On a portion of another wall was a collage of photos and Presley magazine covers. A locked wood cabinet was beside that. Grissom produced a key and opened it. He reached in and handed me a small, clear, film canister with what looked like a toenail in it. "I found it in shag carpet at Graceland," Grissom said, his eyes wild. "I don't know if it's his."

I almost couldn't take it all in.

As I tried to, I abruptly came to wonder something. How did the serious nurse-wife-mother pictured in the living room family portrait cope with her spouse's Elvis obsession? That needed to be in my story. But she was out, Grissom had explained earlier and he didn't know when she would be back. So, though I suddenly had many more questions, I first asked how his wife lived with a closet Elvis kook like him.

He only smiled at this question – warmly this time.

"She's a Barbara Streisand fan," he said. Then, he looked from me to a closed door that I had walked past and taken no note of; it was just before the wax figure Elvises.

"Do you want to see her Barbara Streisand room?" he said.

Phil Andrews was the Managing Editor of the *Guelph Mercury* from September 2005 until the paper's close in January 2016. Prior to coming to Guelph for the *Mercury* job, he had worked at CBC Radio, *The Chronicle-Journal, The Sudbury Star*, and *The New Brunswick Telegraph-Journal*. He now works as a communications consultant with the Ontario Ministry of Agriculture, Food and Rural Affairs.

One of the Boys

Maggie Petrushevsky

"Piece of crap." Glaring at the painting leaning against the credenza beside his desk, Mayor Harkness made a rude sound and swallowed a third of the champagne in his glass. "And I'm supposed to be honoured to get it."

"Better you than me, buddy." Bouchard chuckled. "I'd sue for damage to my environment."

"Did council actually *buy* that eyesore?" Tennyson added, waving his half-empty glass.

The artist's name discreetly printed in the corner of the picture contradicted their unflattering opinions.

Al Lobodici, head of Lobodici Construction, sipped in silence. He rather liked the brilliant reds and blues, although he wasn't sure what that stark black cross in the upper left represented.

Of course, he'd been raised on a farm on the outskirts of Naples, left school at fourteen, emigrated at eighteen. Unlike his companions, he'd been educated only in the values of hard, physical labour. If they saw no merit in the piece, Al presumed they knew something he didn't.

Harkness slugged back the remains of his drink and tossed the plastic glass into the wastebasket. "Thanks for coming, boys. Guess it's time I locked up."

The first man through the door, Al almost collided with a slim, dark-haired woman pushing a wide mop. With her eyes on the floor looking for trash and stray cups left by the crowd attending the official opening of Esquesing's new city hall, she hadn't noticed the quartet.

"Oh." She started and almost dropped her mop handle.

There were more words, but Al didn't understand them. Jeans, a dingy t-shirt, and hair confined by a kerchief identified her as one of the cleaning staff. She looked frightened. Al wanted to reassure her but he knew words wouldn't work. He'd arrived with minimal English and understood how little those strange-sounding syllables meant in the beginning.

He smiled. "Okay," he said. "It's okay."

Her gaze went over his shoulder. Was she nervous of being alone in a building with four men? Her knuckles showed white against the mop's blue wooden handle.

While the mayor closed his door, Bouchard dropped his now-empty glass in front of the mop. Tennyson chuckled. Al glanced back, wondering at his friend's amusement.

"You want rid of that monstrosity, Pete? I think I just got you a solution. Give it to the cleaner." Al figured Tennyson must have drunk two glasses of wine to every one of his.

Three men in dark business suits stared at the fourth. Was he mad?

"Who's she gonna tell?" he continued. "Look at her. Scared to death. She won't talk. And if she does, who'll believe her? Give her the friggin' thing and be rid of it. Can't hurt anyone."

Al knew he had that right. No one believed an immigrant. Especially one who couldn't speak English. And if she did point the finger? At the mayor, a lawyer, an accountant, and a building contractor?

The mayor's eyes sparkled and he chortled. "Damn, you're good." He opened his door and flipped the light switch. In seconds he was back, clutching the large canvas.

"Vida, this is for you."

Vida? Al wondered how he knew her name. But Pete was a politician and politicians remembered things like names.

Vida backed away. The fear in her eyes morphed into suspicion. Still clutching her mop, she pressed her back to the wall, shaking her head, whispering "ne, ne."

Harkeness insisted. "Take it. You work hard. You do a great job. You deserve a little extra."

Five minutes of coaxing and cajoling earned the men nothing. Finally, Harkness turned to where Al stood just beyond the group. "Talk to her, for Chrissake. You were an immigrant once."

"She ain't Italian, Pete," Al snapped. Sometimes the man was a jerk. Still, being part of the mayor's circle gave Al social standing and certain advantages when the town called tenders.

He moved between Vida and the grinning trio. Six-foot-three, 270 pounds, he towered over her. She began to shake.

He put out a big hand and very slowly, very carefully unwrapped her fingers from the mop handle. Using his softest voice and gentlest tone, he told her things would be all right. He saw his words only increased her fears.

He reached back and Harkness thrust the painting into his hand. Al closed Vida's fingers onto the frame, patted her arm, and smiled at her. Now she was bewildered.

She shook her head and frowned. "Ne."

"Yes," Al said. "It's for you."

"Good man. Atta boy." His friends voiced their approval. Harkness clapped a hand to Al's shoulder. Al reassured himself no one would ever know.

Vida was mopping the last few feet of the front hall when the four left the building, still laughing.

"Twenty bucks says it'll take a week before anyone even notices it's gone," Bouchard quipped as they climbed into their cars.

In fact, a month passed before Al heard anything about *Justice*, the painting mysteriously stolen from the mayor's office.

Justice? What was that about? His secretary, Jill, enlightened him.

"That white upright is Lady Justice. The black crossbar is her scale," she said. "The red and blue are from the flag of our British background."

"Oh," was Al's brilliant response.

"Seems the cleaning lady stole it," Jill continued. "Claims it was given to her. As if! A genuine $7,500 Theordore Blakmint?"

Al's morning coffee burned his stomach ulcer. Shit. They said no one would get hurt. The cops must be investigating. His voice unsteady, he asked how the painting had been found.

"Silly fool threw it in her garbage. Said the mayor gave it to her. Can you imagine?" The secretary rolled her eyes.

Horrified, Al handed Jill the details to start writing their new contract and disappeared back into his office.

What in hell should they do? Get a lawyer? If Vida went to court she was bound to blame them. And so she should. She didn't steal the painting. They just hadn't expected her to dump it. But then, she didn't understand English. Christ what a mess.

It was 8:15 a.m. Al punched Harkness' number into his phone. The answering machine picked up. Damn. Should he go to the house?

His nine o'clock planning department meeting couldn't be cancelled.

Bouchard was probably still home. Mrs. Bouchard recognized Al's voice and went to get her husband.

Al couldn't hear the words, just the rumble of voices. She sounded embarrassed when she came back.

"Sorry about that Mr. Lobodici. You just missed him."

Tennyson cut Al off the moment he heard his voice.

"Nothing to talk about. The stupid broad brought it on herself. All she had to do was keep the damned thing out of sight. Now she's trying to blame us."

"Because we gave it to her," Al pointed out.

"Doesn't matter. The cops caught her. It's her problem. We just keep quiet."

"But…"

"No buts. I'm serious, Al. This could ruin us. Pete's in politics. Might not be re-elected next year anyway. But us? My customers depend on me to keep their books straight. One whiff of irregularities and they'll vanish. Bouchard's, too. Who deals with a shady lawyer?"

"And Vida?" Al spluttered. "What about her? She could be deported for all we know."

"Is that her name?" Tennyson wasn't interested. "She pinched it. The police nailed her. Leave well enough alone if you know what's good for you."

"If I know what's good for me?" Al was indignant. Was Tennyson threatening him?

"You're a wop, Al. The mob is full of wops. Cops know that. A big-time Italian contractor and a refugee from some country where girls hit the streets because there's no honest work available? How would that look if the press got hold of it?"

Words stuck in Al's throat. His heart hammered and he shook so hard his chair rattled.

"Just keep your mouth shut," Tennyson repeated. "She's been charged. It'll be over soon."

"Have the police questioned you?" Al asked.

"No."

"Why not?"

"Why should they, for Chrissake? I'm a reputable businessman. Trashy no-names like her point fingers at professionals like me all the time. The cops know that."

"I see." And he did see – a conniving bastard determined to save his own skin regardless of the cost to his victim.

Al slammed down the receiver and took off for the town office in his truck.

His mind consumed with visions of the frightened woman, Al only heard bits of the planning staffer's comments. When the meeting finished, he drove directly to Bouchard's office and found him getting out of his car. The lawyer's jaw muscles tightened when Al followed him up the building's steps.

Al took a wild guess. "The cops questioned you, didn't they?"

Bouchard nodded. "Yeah. But I have a solid alibi."

"Right. Us."

"Exactly. And so have you, if they talk to you," Bouchard added. "All our reputations are on the line here. It was just a joke, for God's sake. Who knew the piece of crap was valuable. A masterpiece, for crying out loud? More like something turned out by a dog with a paint brush tied to its tail."

Now they were in the hall in front of Bouchard's office suite. He heaved on the oak door and held it open with his foot.

"Maybe we should pay for Vida's lawyer," Al suggested.

Bouchard's attention snapped to Al's face. "Are you crazy? How would that make us look?"

"It's the least we can do. She can't afford a good lawyer."

"Don't be stupid."

Al stepped forward.

Bouchard held out an arm. "No. We'll talk another day."

There was only one other participant to approach. Al drove to City Hall. Harkness' private parking space was empty. Al checked his watch. It was 11:45. Having an early lunch at the South Esquesing Golf and Country Club? He turned around and drove across town. The Mayor's Cadillac occupied a reserved spot near the dining room's main entrance.

Normally, Harkness gestured at the chair across the table and invited Al to join him. Today his glare was frosty.

Al ignored the hostile expression and sat. No time for pleasantries. "Have the police talked to you?"

The mayor set down his water glass, his eyes narrowing. "This is not the time or place."

"So they have. What did you tell them?"

"Nothing." Harkness leaned forward. "It was a joke. It went wrong. There's nothing we can do. Too bad."

"Nothing?" Al sputtered. "She's facing –"

"Leave it." Harkness' voice cracked like a drill sergeants. Realizing he'd spoken too loudly, he glanced about, then leaned back. "It's done, Al. I'm sorry, but that's it. We don't get involved."

Al stared at his friend for several long seconds before getting to his feet. He leaned over the table, ignoring a waiter a foot away. "No, Mr. Mayor, it is not done."

Back in his truck, Al contemplated the view. Single-storey stuccoed clubhouse with brick quoins. Lonely dwarf spruce strategically placed in the still-bare flowerbeds. Behind the building the golf greens showed only pre-spring brown. Big willows trailed graceful branches down to the creek. His spirit wept for the welcome he'd never again receive in this place he'd enjoyed so much.

He put the truck in gear, started back along the main street to the cop shop, five blocks away.

How hard he'd worked to get a job. To learn the language. To fit in. All the while keeping his nose clean. Refusing shortcuts with dubious rewards. He'd succeeded, too. A nice home, a successful business, a solid reputation, friends in key places. It was a good life. The sort of life Vida doubtless wanted. And would never have unless he dredged up the courage of his youth. The courage not to be just another one of the boys.

Maggie Petrushevsky's byline first appeared on *The Daily Mercury*'s District Page when she took over *The Mercury*'s one-person Acton Bureau, in January 1980. With Erin and Eramosa Townships and the Town of Halton Hills as her personal bailiwick, she spent the first seven years of her *Mercury* life at schools, community events, political campaigns of all stripes and levels, a minimum of seven council meetings a month, school board meetings, and more fires and vehicle accidents than she can remember. She later served in the Guelph newsroom, pulling five years on the Women's Page under Rosemary Anderson and as long a spell handling the weekly food page. After the strike in 1992, Maggie was returned to the city-side weekend duty rotation and wound up as the only reporter on the ground immediately after the tornado struck Arthur at the end of her shift on the final Saturday of April, 1996. She left the *Mercury* that August. Family health issues forced her to take a year off before joining the first staff, part-time at the fledgling *New Acton Tanner*, in January 1998. That was when she also began taking notes for deaf University of Toronto students in Mississauga. She left *The Tanner* in 2006 and retired from note taking in 2015. She has produced two novels under her pen name Maggie Petru, both published by Guelph's Sun Dragon Press and available through Amazon.ca or her website, Maggiepetru.com

Baba Turns Her Ring

Ben Gelinas

The paved road north of the village stops abruptly and becomes old gravel. Anna's mother swerves as her car finds its feet in the dirt. Only a hiccup, but Anna gasps from the passenger side – residual shock from a car crash a couple years ago that took the hearing in her right ear and a hell of a lot of happiness.

Philly puts a hand on Anna's shoulder from the backseat. She smiles and he doesn't see it.

"So how are you finding life out here, Philly?" Anna's mother asks, keeping her eyes on the road.

Philly takes a second to answer.

"It's...different, Mrs. Fyodorov," he says, careful not to rant about how much it actually bugs him: The explicit judgement of the predominantly French-Catholic townies. The strange customs of the 'White Russians', an ultraorthodox community of Old Believers on the outskirts, to which Anna and her mother both belong.

"It's not like back home."

He hates everything about their weird town – and everyone in it except Anna.

"Anna tells me you're from a much bigger place? Five thousand people?"

"Six thousand," Philly says.

"That's a lot more than the two hundred and fifty in the village. You probably had more kids in your high school than we have all together."

"Yeah," Philly says, leaving it at that.

Anna and her mother are wearing matching dresses. Ankle-length bulk fabric. Their heads, hands, and boots poke out from galaxies of small pink roses floating in powder blue. Anna's mother wears a matching headscarf because she's married.

Mrs. Fyodorov made the dresses. Old Believers are supposed to make all their own clothes, though they draw the line at things like underwear and shoes. In gym class, the boys wear Adidas shorts, same as Philly.

The girls stay in their dresses though.

"Are you nervous, Philly?" Anna's mother asks. "To meet Anna's baba?"

"Not really," Philly says. "I tend to get along with old people. Old people and dogs."

"My baba's not like most old people...or dogs," Anna says.

"Anna!" her mother says.

"Well, she's not."

Anna turns her attention back to the window as her mother mutters something in Russian. The prairie fields and conifer trees are on a loop: the same dusty hay bales and cows congregate over and over. Afternoon sun hits Anna's blonde braids and makes them shine like brass. Scant strands peeking out the front of her mother's headscarf look much the same; but beyond the clothes and hair, the pair couldn't be more different.

Anna's mother married at seventeen and immediately dropped out of school. She had her first kid, a shithead named Alexander, at eighteen. Anna's her fourth of seven children, and absolutely the trouble-maker. They're still dealing with the fallout from Anna telling her father she wants to go to university next year – for political science of all things.

"Wouldn't you rather get married?" her father asked, and asks her almost daily.

This isn't to say Anna's family is particularly orthodox. They disobey the church where it matters. Two of her brothers are already in college. Though idle entertainment is forbidden, there's a pretty good television in their living room that they throw a tablecloth over when elders visit. The satellite dish is hidden in the trees behind a shed on the acreage. They don't eat meat for months at a time, but Oreos are all well and good during the fast. No meat or dairy in those.

Philly feels his face. He shaved it this morning – what little grows, anyway. He wonders if Anna's baba will be offended. White Russian men aren't supposed to shave their faces. Clothing aside, you can spot the Russian boys at school by the bad facial hair.

"What do you think your baba will think of me?" Philly asks, breaking a bit of silence.

"Honestly, I think she'll worry we're dating," Anna says.

"I already told her you're just friends, Anna. Don't worry," her mother says. "But are you dating?"

"Mom!"

"What? I wouldn't be upset if you are." Anna shifts awkwardly in her seat. "All I ask is that you try to keep something like that quiet. It's not like your father would approve."

"Or God?"

"Or God."

Philly slinks down deeper into the backseat of the Buick. There's a lot of seat to hide in. Sun gets in his eyes and he uses the excuse to rest them rather than keep the conversation going.

Soon, they pull up the drive to Baba's. There's no doorbell and Anna's mother doesn't bother to knock. She won't hear anyway.

Inside, the house is immaculately kept, if musty and dim – like an old library, except there's very little of anything. Simple, hand-made furniture. A galley kitchen with orange appliances. Green carpet, thick as wool. The air smells like cabbage. Philly wonders if Baba's cooked a meal, then decides it must always smell this way.

As Baba approaches her visitors, Anna's mother introduces Philly in Russian. He doesn't quite understand what she says, but nods at the old woman and says: "Pleased to meet you."

Baba grunts and leads them to the living room, where she's laid out some fresh baked bread, three glasses, and a pitcher of well water.

There's a purple gift bag too, at the foot of the coffee table. Baba slowly lifts it from the carpet and hands the bag to Anna. Inside, there are shoes: worn, black Mary Janes. They look way too small for Anna's feet.

She smiles and thanks her baba for the gift.

"Mom grew up so poor. Nine brothers and sisters," Anna's mother says. "They had to fight over who got to wear shoes."

Philly inspects the old woman as she eases into her armchair and won't notice him staring. Thin eyes. Firm hump. Her skin seemingly dead but hanging on. Baba's headscarf is white and fixed farther back than most, showing thinning hair with no brass. It's more like scuffed silver.

"She had her first piece of chocolate at sixteen," Anna's mother explains. "She threw up. It was too rich."

Philly believes it.

This woman, who Anna says crossed from Russia to China under persecution, reaching Australia by boat and finally settling in Western Canada. This woman doesn't need chocolate. At 89, she still tends chickens. Still lives the way she wants. And she'll probably die this way too, Philly thinks: in her home, because it's a way to go. It's not special. But it's a way to go. As she sits, listening to her daughter speak English to this non-believer in a T-shirt, Baba turns over a solitary ring on her finger. A simple band, tarnished and bent. It's weak gold if it's gold at all.

Baba is so thin she wears a Band-Aid underneath to keep the ring from slipping off. Philly wonders if it's a wedding ring. He's noticed that Anna's mother doesn't seem wear one.

Anna's mother rises and pours a glass of water for herself, handing the others to Baba and Anna.

"May I have some water, please?" Philly asks, careful to be polite. Anna nods and starts to the kitchen for a fourth glass.

"Wait, Anna," her mom says, stopping her. "Baba won't like Philly drinking out of her glasses."

"Of course she won't, but what, we let him go thirsty?" Anna says. She seems annoyed.

"What's wrong?" Philly asks. "Did I do something wrong?"

"It's just frowned upon," Anna's mom says. "In our church, non-believers are seen as...how can I put this without offending, Philly?"

"Unclean," Anna says from the kitchen. "You're dirty. You live a dirty life. So we're not supposed to share anything with you. Glasses. Forks. Even plates. It's weird, I know."

"Like germs?" Philly asks.

"Sort of," Anna's mom says. "Only religious."

Baba has a permanent scowl on her face. It's not clear that she understands what anyone is saying.

"It's fine," Philly says. "I'm okay without water. I have a bottle of pop in the car. I'll just drink that when we go."

"You sure?" Anna says. "It'll be warm." She obviously feels pretty bad about this. Embarrassed even.

"Yeah. No worries. Really."

Outside, a rooster calls. Philly learned recently that that doesn't just happen at dawn. Philly's learned a lot of things since moving here.

He decides that Baba's house smells like hot yeast and cabbage. There is definitely no television covered in tablecloth. No radio either. He spots a few books – none in English. There is a clock in the kitchen. It ticks loudly, working hard to fill the silence as Anna returns to her seat.

"You really should know better," Anna's mother says. "Should I, Mother?" Anna is not happy. Her mother is not happy. Philly is not sure what to say. Baba turns her ring.

"You're not a child anymore, Anniska. At your age, I was married. And your baba already had your uncle Vasily."

"And you're wondering what I've done?"

"I didn't say that."

"I guess caring about school makes me a bad kid?"

"I didn't say that either."

"A bad woman, then. Because I didn't bend over from some neighbour's son with pubes on his face?"

"Anna!"

Anna stands up, this time with force, and stomps into the kitchen. She grabs a glass from the cupboard, turns on the tap and fills it. Stomping back into the living room, she pointedly hands it to Philly.

"Here," she says. "Drink it."

Philly looks at the cloudy water. The glass is thick and warm in his hands. He looks up at Anna's mother, flush with anger, and then at Anna, whose face looks much the same.

"I'd better not, Anna."

He places it on the table.

"Unbelievable," Anna says.

"I'll be in the car."

She slams the front door and is gone.

Her mother shakes her head, as Philly tries and fails to sink deeper into the rigid couch. Baba turns her ring.

Ben Gelinas interned at the *Guelph Mercury* newsroom in the summer of 2006, and went on to cover crime and the arts at the *Edmonton Journal* before callously turning his back on the noble craft of journalism to make video games at BioWare. He misses reporting, but says there's a quiet dignity in getting paid to tell elves and space aliens what to do.

Bramasole

Alex Migdal

The house, as you stagger up the gravel road, looms large and proud. Without warning, miles of gravel and foliage give way to a man-made marvel.

You might notice the manicured hedges lining the staircase. Or the colossal slab of stone on which the three-storey house rests. I spot the green shutters, which pop against the wall of muted pink and gold.

This is Bramasole.

For many, this home is their dreamscape of Tuscany, of terraced hills and olive oil, of warm breezes and chiming clock towers. Busloads of tourists, mostly female and ornamented in sun hats and sheer scarves, embark every day on the two-kilometre trek from Cortona.

These pilgrims are here for Tuscany's version of the Vatican City. And their patron saint is Frances Mayes.

Since the publication of her 1995 memoir, *Under the Tuscan Sun*, Mayes has cast a rosy light on what she calls the most "civilized" town on the globe. Five years earlier, the writer famously stumbled on a neglected 200-year-old Tuscan farmhouse nestled in five unkempt acres of Cortona. Her home renovation became the plot of her bestselling memoir and inspired droves of young women to pursue similar quests of self-discovery. Mayes maintains that enthusiasts still regularly visit the house.

"I'm at my window right now and I can see three of them," she told The Telegraph newspaper in a 2010 phone interview.

But right now, Mayes is nowhere to be found.

In her place are two workers lifting and reconfiguring stone blocks like a game of Tetris. Their skins are leathery and charred. Blobs of sweat stain their white t-shirts. They frown as I step onto the entryway.

"No, no," they shout.

The men drop their shovels and motion for me to back up.

I point to the house. At the top of the stairs, steps from the door, stands a middle-aged couple. A map pokes out of the women's hand. The man is tall and silver-haired, his arm draped around the woman's shoulder. They appear entranced by the space.

"What about them?" I ask.

The woman peers down and waves. Her smile is soft and modest, etching crinkles on her cheeks. Her blouse, a regal pink, matches the house.

The workers wave back with disciplined smiles, then turn to me and grunt. Suddenly, I hear a chorus of Italian, weighed down by a Southern drawl.

The woman descends the stairs and points to a lopsided lemon tree. The workers nod eagerly. As she strolls away, the workers shoot me a knowing look and make a scribbling motion.

"Autograph," the heavier worker says in a thick accent.

Their employer, I realize, is Frances Mayes.

* * * * *

Affixed to the stone wall of the Piazzetta Pescheria is a sign that details the loggia's architecture and history. The front stone parapet, the sign notes, was built between the end of the seventeenth and the start of the eighteenth century. It now overlooks Piazza della Repubblica, Cortona's main square and the nucleus of this remote Tuscan town.

Beneath the passage is a quote from *Under the Tuscan Sun*:

> *From here, you can see a loggia on the level above across the piazzo, where the fish market used to be. Now it's terrace seating for a restaurant and another perch for viewing.*

I study the flowery lettering on the sign post: "An Enchanting Walk *Under the Tuscan Sun*." Mayes's passage is accompanied by a still from the 2003 film. It shows Diane Lane, who plays Mayes despite sharing little in appearance, and a smitten Italian man sitting on the stone parapet. They are flanked by pots of blooming flowers. Clay roofs behind them dot an oversaturated blue sky.

More than a decade later, charcoal clouds obscure the May sun. A gang of pigeons circle above in a screeching vortex as the growl of construction work slices through the piazza.

To the left of the pictured spot is the weathered wall of the two-arched terrace. It is an easel for deviant minds. "Out House" is inscribed twice in shaky toddler scrawl, punctuated with twisted pigeon feathers. Two Italians in bug-eyed sunglasses saunter by and tap their cigarette butts on the commemorated spot.

Unlike Diane Lane and her romantic interest, the couples in the piazza are fixated on its winding streets and impossible design. One man in mint-green pants drowns in his map. His wife's eyes are ringed with purple bags. She sprawls over the steps of the fourteenth century City Hall and lifelessly scoops her gelato. For minutes, neither shares a word.

Another couple, hunchbacked with swollen camera bags, stops to read the sign post. Realizing their discovery, the woman asks the man to photograph her. She sits on the stone parapet, the same spot on which Diane Lane was once wooed over innumerable takes.

The camera's shutter clicks and the man turns his lens to the piazza. The woman, unaware of her partner's new pursuit, sits still, her fragile smile frozen.

* * * * *

Frances Mayes will never fully commit to Tuscany.

She may be its most revered muse, a conjurer of airy portraits, the enchantress of mythical, sun-bathed havens, but her love affair with Italy is not monogamous.

Mayes splits her year between Cortona, the hillside town she made famous, and North Carolina.

"My husband would move there in a moment, but I like living here just as well," she told a journalist a few years ago in North Carolina.

"I like my American life. I like going to bookstores and seeing my friends. I'm an American, so I would not permanently decamp to another country. But I feel lucky to have two cultures because it's interesting the way they bounce off each other for us."

Mayes and her husband have flown back and forth so many times that they are now recognized by flight attendants and customs officers.

To have two homes, to be immersed in two cultures, is a rare gift. But it's not unusual in Italy. Mayes has said about 20 expats have bought homes near Bramasole.

How could they not?

The day I journeyed to the famed house, the sky was so blue, the air so sweet and pleasant, and the tended fields so rousing that I couldn't help but panic at the thought of leaving.

* * * * *

The night after I found Bramasole, I hardly slept.

My body was tense, my mind heavy. In two days, I would be flying to Toronto. I studied my watch as the arm slid past 4 a.m. I thought of the time zone change, of having to rewind six hours and fall behind, not just in time, but in a way of life.

For hours, I debated whether to go. The trip wasn't in vain. I was to be given a prestigious journalism award. The month before I left, I had processed the news in disbelief, in awe that someone had found merit in my stories.

But I had resigned myself to not going. Logistically, it was tricky. And the trust fund had politely declined to cover my international airfare. That finalized the decision. I would stay in Italy and revel in my nomadic life, where, to my relief, no one ever asked about my career.

The email two days ago had changed that. The trust fund had scraped together some last-minute funds and would be delighted if I could attend not the luncheon initially planned, but the black-tie gala that would celebrate the country's top journalists.

"You have to go. Imagine all the people you'll meet," my mom had pleaded over a string of phone calls.

As I lay in bed, I resisted any dreamy notion of the gala. I thought of all the gelato I had yet to taste, of the trains I could ride, of the art I wanted to admire.

I would call the airline tomorrow and cancel the trip.

I fell asleep thinking about my newly planned weekend, rowing through a winding canal in Venice under a starry sky.

* * * * *

"So, what do you do?"

I paused as I observed the congestion of cars outside the window.

"I'm...a student," I said. "Just here to visit friends for the weekend."

The tattooed hair stylist smacked her gum and nodded. "Cool. Where are you from?"

"Edmonton." I smiled. "Just flew in yesterday."

Without response, she spritzed a sheet of mist and combed my hair. Brown locks began to fall like flurries.

I had said little since landing in Toronto that morning. Other than obligatory answers to the bus driver, the concierge and the gala coordinator, there wasn't much to say, even in English.

Frances Mayes was once asked if she ever felt Italian.

"Oh no, I wish I could, but no, I don't. I'm kind of a quiet person, and I feel like there, I have become a lot less reserved and I certainly gesture with my hands a lot more than I used to," she said.

"And I know that I've absorbed a lot of their attitudes and ways of being, but I still feel first of all Southern and second of all American."

Mayes said she felt metabolically Southern. Here, I felt superficially Canadian, like a passing neighbour forced to stay for coffee.

I studied the spire of the CN Tower outside the window. The landscape seemed drab and utilitarian, a mangled mix of concrete and glass.

I found it silly here to gesture my hands. The question "How are you?" seemed benign and the brisk pace of suited downtowners annoyed me.

The city lacked the warmth I craved. Mayes, too, had noticed this.

"I find that other countries have this or this, but Italy is the only one that has it all for me," she said. "The culture, the cuisine, the people, the landscape, the history. Just everything to me comes together there."

Everything to me comes together there. I had tried many times to come up with descriptions about Italy for friends and family, but all I could muster were superlatives: Beautiful, warm, perfect.

But finally, a fitting statement. Italy: A place of synthesis.

* * * * *

Frances Mayes is nervous as we speak.

I've just told her about my spring semester in Cortona and confessed my admiration for her work. She has shaken my hand and smiled and nodded politely, all the social cues expected of a gracious Southern woman.

But a van has suddenly rolled up and tourists are ogling the woman who has supplied them with years of literary fantasies.

Glancing timidly behind my shoulder, she tells me she's just recently arrived to Cortona for the summer. I ask whether she's still teaching creative writing in San Francisco.

"No, I quit this year," she sighs. "Thank goodness."

She doesn't disclose details, but I'm reminded of her frayed relationship with Cortona.

Several years ago, she and her husband protested the installation of a pool near their farmhouse. The editor of the local newspaper slammed her interference and a group of residents turned against her. She awoke one day to a grenade in her garden. Like the growing crack in her farmhouse, which tourists have observed with sadness, Mayes has come to acknowledge the blurring of myth and reality.

"The reverberations of that time are still going on," she told a reporter.

As I say goodbye to Mayes, I notice the map in her hands. It's nearly crumpled in her clenched fist. She poses for an awkward photo with a fawning woman from New Jersey. I wonder whether the film of sweat on Mayes' forehead is from the sun or the tourists.

I approach Bramasole to get one last look. The van's engine is revving and the workers' jackhammer is growling and the house is suddenly shielded by a swirling cloud of dust.

I look back and Mayes is gone.

Alex Migdal was a reporter for the *Guelph Mercury* in 2014. During his summer stint, he reported on the provincial election and the City of Guelph's transit lockdown, and produced an investigative feature on Ontario's driving legislation. He won an Ontario Newspaper Award and the Goff Penny Award for Canada's best young journalist. Alex has since worked as a national reporter for *The Globe and Mail*. He's now a student at the UBC Graduate School of Journalism in Vancouver, specializing in media studies and cultural journalism.

The Stop

Michael Troy Bridgeman

"Thermals rise and fall carrying the sweet fragrance of flowers and fruit-tree blossoms over the rolling vineyards and olive groves of Tuscany."

Chris pauses to take in the scenery, then continues writing.

"The Renaissance Art tour, though a little too regimented for my taste, has been educational and inspirational."

"Day Three, began in Rome, at 6 a.m. and whisked us through several medieval towns and basilicas. By 2 p.m. most of the others, including my girlfriend Victoria, who is nestled comfortably under my arm, are exhausted and asleep."

Chris yawns and wipes the sweat from his forehead.

Passengers at the front were cold so they turned off the air conditioning creating the perfect conditions for dozing off. The two glasses of Chianti he had at their lunch stop and the rocking of the bus, as it navigates the winding mountain roads, are the *fait accompli.*

Within minutes of closing his eyes he is jolted awake as the bus slows down to make a sharp turn. The movement rouses several more passengers, their eyes red and their hair stuck to their face.

"I'm a so sorry to disturba you," says tour guide Stefania in a raspy Venetian accent. "I see many of you were sleeping, butta there has beena somma problems with the bussa and we have a to make an un-scheduled stoppa."

The weary passengers mumble to their travelling companions.

Chris slips the notebook into his camera bag and checks his watch – 2:17 p.m.

"We'll be lucky if we get to Florence before dark."

Stefania continues. "I've phoned ahead and arranged some rooms for you in a charming little hotella where you canna shower, if you like and relax untilla the problem is corrected. Of course, the rooma and all services are free of a charge."

The bus climbs a steep road that circles like a corkscrew toward the peak of a small mountain. As they ascend, a large, medieval fortress comes into view. Its fortifications encircle the summit with a twelve storey tower rising from the centre.

A massive door opens allowing the bus to drive through the thick, stone, wall and into an expansive courtyard well populated with marble sculptures of citizens enjoying a day in the countryside.

"What is this place?" Chris asks, staring out the large tinted window?

"The Canto Dodici Hotel," says another passenger, reading from a sign.

Everyone looks around in fascination as uniformed porters, with military precision, take their bags and lead them to their respective rooms.

Chris and Victoria are delighted to find their luxury suite furnished with a tasteful combination of antique and modern furniture.

Portage gratuities were included in the tour package but Chris, instinctively, tipped anyway. This is the first time a porter politely declined.

"*No grazie. Tutto va bene*," the porter says, with a smile. "*Sono ricco.*"

Victoria smiles. "He said he's already rich."

"Oh, *si*," says Chris. "*Grazie.*"

"*Prego*," says the porter. "*Buon giorno.*"

"*Buon giorno*," says Chris, as the porter leaves. "This place will definitely get a good review."

Victoria sprawls out on the satin sheets of the king-size bed. "If the last hotel was a four-star, this is easily an eight."

Chris laughs, "They only go to five."

"Have you ever stayed in a place this nice?" she asks.

He thinks for a second. "No."

"This suite is bigger than our house."

She jumps up and walks into the bathroom. "Check it out."

Solid gold fixtures brilliantly reflect off the polished marble floor and walls. The giant, claw-foot tub is, easily, big enough for two or more.

"I'm running a bath," she says. "Care to join me?"

"I'll pour us some wine," he says.

After their bath, they order from room service. Again, the tip is politely declined.

"I could get used to this," says Chris, carving into his steak Florentine.

"It would be a shame if we had to stay here overnight."

"Maybe I should sneak down and sabotage the bus," he says.

Victoria raises her glass. "*Viva Italia.*"

"*Salute*," Chris replies.

Around 5 p.m., there is a knock on the door. It is Stefania, the tour director, who invites them to join her and the others on the observation deck on top of the tower.

After everyone is assembled, several soldiers march on to the deck followed by an officer who steps up to a microphone-bearing podium.

"*Buona sera.* My name is Captain Michelangelo Della Scalla and it is my duty to inform you that we are doing an investigation. I know you are all eager to continue your tour. So, in the interest of expediency, we expect everyone's full cooperation."

As he speaks, soldiers secure the exits and take positions along the wall of the circular deck.

"We have set up several tables. We ask that you find the table with your name and sit down where you will be required to answer some questions."

The stunned tourists, seeing little recourse, nervously, comply.

Victoria grabs Chris's arm and whispers through the side of her mouth as they walk. "You didn't bring any weed with you?"

"No."

"You didn't buy any here?"

"No."

"What about that book you bought?"

"What book?"

94

Before she can elaborate, they come to a table reserved for Victoria Allegheri. She looks nervously at the interrogator and then to Chris.

"Just tell them the truth," Chris tells her. "You've got nothing to hide."

He walks another ten meters to the next table, which is reserved for Christopher Mitchum. A stern man with a laptop gestures for Chris to sit across from him.

"Passport," says the man.

Chris hands it over.

The man glances back and forth between Chris and his passport photo. "That was three years ago," says Chris. "I cut my hair and grew a mustache since. My girlfriend thinks it makes me look older. I told her I'll shave it off as soon as we get back to Canada."

"What is the purpose of your visit to Italy?" asks the interrogator.

Chris shrugs and says: "Vacation."

"Did you bring any illegal contraband into the country?"

"No," says Chris, concluding it is probably best to give one-word answers and say as little as possible.

"Are you carrying any weapons or illegal drugs?"

"No."

"What cities have you visited?"

"We landed in Rome and today we visited Sienna."

"That's it?"

"So far," says Chris. "Yes."

The interrogator frowns and looks into Chris's eyes. "Just Rome and Sienna."

"That's right," Chris responds.

"What about Vatican City?" asks the interrogator.

"*Si*, yes, yes," says Chris. "We went to the Vatican."

The interrogator squints momentarily in annoyance. "Why didn't you tell me that when I asked?"

"The Vatican is in Rome. I told you we visited Rome."

"Vatican City is not only a separate city, it is a separate country."

"I understand that," says Chris nervously. "I just thought…"

"You are a Roman Catholic." The interrogator cuts him off and reads from the laptop screen.

"That's right," says Chris, craning his neck to get a look at the screen.

The interrogator turns the screen so Chris can't see. "Confirmation name is Michael."

"How do you know that?" Chris chuckles. "Why do you know that?"

"You are travelling with Victoria Allegheri?"

"I'm travelling with my fiancée, Victoria," he says glancing over at her.

"So, you are not married."

Chris notices Victoria glancing nervously back at him. "No, not yet."

"But, you sleep together, in the same bed."

"We've been living together for six years."

"When you were in Vatican City, did you visit the Sistine Chapel?"

"Yes, we did."

"Did you take anything from the Chapel?"

"What do you mean," asks Chris?

"Did you take anything that didn't belong to you?"

"No," says Chris. "Nothing."

The interrogator swings the laptop around, allowing Chris to see surveillance footage of him and Victoria in the Sistine Chapel.

"Did you not read the signs or hear the curator announce that taking video and photographs was strictly prohibited?"

"But everyone was…"

The interrogator places Chris's notebook on the table. "Why are you making detailed notes about train schedules, bus routes and all kinds of other suspicious entries?"

"How did you get that?" Chris says, his voice rising as both outrage and apprehension seize him.

"Answer the question," the interrogator demands.

"I'm making notes for a travel story."

"You are a journalist?"

"That's right," says Chris. In futility, he then removes his wallet and searches for his press credentials but quickly recalls that he cleaned out any unneeded ID from the billfold before leaving on the trip.

"You can call my boss in Toronto. She'll confirm what I'm saying."

"Why are you attempting to conceal your identity?"

"I'm not."

"You didn't tell the airline officials or your tour director that you were a journalist."

"When you are a restaurant critic you don't tell the waitress. Same thing goes with travel writers. I want to get the same treatment as the shmuck next to me."

"What is 'shmuck'?"

"You know," says Chris, desperately. "Just a regular guy. No one special."

"So, you are special?"

"No, that's not what I mean. They are more likely to give me special treatment if they know I'm writing a review."

The interrogator places Chris's camera bag on the table. "We will need some time to go over your notes, view your photographs and confirm your identity. You will wait in your room until then."

Chris looks to Victoria but her back is to him. Two armed guards step forward and escort him to his room.

He tries to make a phone call but is told there are no outside lines. Worst-case scenarios race through his mind as he paces in the empty suite.

He is relieved when Victoria returns.

"Holy shit, Vicky? I was beginning to worry."

She is trembling. Her eyes are welled with tears. "I'm really scared."

He is moved by this. She rarely reveals a vulnerable side or exhibits a lack of confidence. But her uncommon presentation also fill him with a quiet trepidation. She is usually his support system in moments of crisis.

He tries to comfort her while masking his own uncertainty. "We're Canadian citizens and Italy is a G8 country. It's not like they're gonna line us up and shoot us."

"They know everything we've done since we got here. They've been watching us or something." She looks at Chris suspiciously. "Why?"

"They have surveillance cameras all over this country," he says. "Maybe they have us confused with someone else."

"They know who we are," she says. "They know all kinds of shit about us."

They are interrupted by a knock. Chris reluctantly opens the door. It is Stefania the tour director.

"I'm a so sorry," she says. "I'm a sure this is just a big misunderstanding."

"What are they looking for?" asks Chris.

"I don't know," she says. "They radioed us and told us there was a problem with the bussa and that we were to proceed to the Canto Dodici Hotel and a wait for authorities to arrive."

"What's wrong with the bus?" asks Victoria.

"I don't know," says Stefania. "*Fuori de servizio.*"

Chris suspects she knows more than she is saying.

"I don't know how long this will take," says Stefania. "I just want to remind you again that all rooma service is a free."

"What about making a phone call to our families?" asks Victoria.

"There's no outside line," says Chris.

"They took my phone," says Victoria.

"I will see what I can arrange. In the meantime, try to relaxa," she says, before closing the door behind her. "*Buona sera.*"

Chris checks the door. It is locked from the outside.

"Maybe there were drugs on the bus," says Victoria.

"Maybe there was a bomb," says Chris. "Maybe they think one of us is a terrorist."

Victoria is dismissive. "Why would a terrorist go on a Renaissance art tour?"

"Where better to hide, than with a bunch of tourists? We've been to some pretty important places with huge political and religious significance."

"But, who? It's crazy. We're probably the most dangerous people in the group."

Chris rummages through his suitcase. "They took my notebook, the cameras."

Victoria opens a window. "We're sure not getting out this way."

A sheer cliff below the window drops four hundred meters to a pile of jagged rocks. The panoramic view of the pastoral curved horizon is spectacular.

"They even took my travel bag with my toothbrush and deodorant," says Chris.

"They must be looking for drugs," says Victoria. "I saw a piece on TV once where they hid heroin in toothpaste tubes."

Chris calls room service. "I'd like to order a tube of toothpaste, a couple toothbrushes, two bottles of your finest champagne and a tray of sushi."

Victoria is cautiously amused. "You think that's a good idea?"

He nods his head and winks. "You want anything?"

"Half a dozen Belgian truffles," she says, grinning mischievously.

"And a dozen Belgian truffles," says Chris. "That's all for now, *grazie*."

Their order arrives and within minutes they're stretched across the bed making short work of the first bottle of champagne.

"It's definitely something to do with terrorism," says Chris, loading his California roll with ginger and wasabi. "We haven't been charged with anything. We're being held without the right to a phone call. If this was a simple criminal investigation…"

"What," asks Victoria, catching a buzz and growing impatient with his know-it-all, "is your rationale?"

Chris is caught off guard by her tone. "It would be different," he says.

"How? We're in Italy. This isn't Canada."

"No, but there are fundamental principles that everyone recognizes. *Habeas corpus* for one. The right to be told why you're being held and, if you're charged, what the charge is." He stuffs the sushi in his mouth and talks with his mouth full. "The right to an attorney."

"But it's different if they think you're a terrorist," says Victoria, popping the cork on the second bottle.

"Exactly," he says.

"You think it's the Brazilians?" she says, sarcastically, referring to a family of five from Sao Paulo. "They've been pretty keep-to-ourselves."

"You never know," he says. "Maybe in an ironic twist, they've resorted to terrorism in protest over one of them being accidentally mistaken for a terrorist."

"Or," says Victoria, "maybe they're not Brazilians at all but Iraqis, cleverly disguised as Brazilians."

"Brilliant cover," says Chris, happy to see her joking around.

Victoria washes a truffle down with a mouthful of champagne. "Maybe it's the honeymooners. There's something suspicious about all that cuddling and handholding. She claims to be Jewish and he claims to be a Filipino Catholic. But that could be just another clever ruse."

"The way she nags and bosses him around is a little too scripted."

"She is definitely the leader of that terrorist cell."

"When he married her he was volunteering for a suicide mission."

He prepares another piece of sushi and has a drink of champagne. "It's the person you'd least suspect."

"What about Ted?"

Chris laughs nearly choking on his food. "He is the antithesis of Osama Bin Laden. He represents everything the terrorists hate. A wealthy, bigoted Texas neocon, who thinks the U.S. is the center of the universe."

"He's perfect," Victoria exclaims.

"Come to think of it," says Chris. "I don't remember Ted getting back on the bus after lunch."

"Have you seen him since we got here?" she asks.

"No."

"That's weird."

"It sure is," says Chris.

They are quiet for a while as they continue to stuff their faces.

"Did you tell them about your criminal record?" she asks.

"No! Are you kidding? I told them as little as possible. Besides that was over twenty-five years ago. I was just a kid."

"Did they ask you about that book?"

"What book?"

"That book about all the conspiracies theories surrounding 9/11. I told you not to buy it."

100

"I'm a journalist. It is my job to collect information. I'm curious how the people over here think about the whole thing."

Victoria gives him a discerning look.

Chris is frustrated. "I don't know why you're making such a fuss about that. It's just a book."

"The Koran is just a book. The Bible is just a book. We came here to get away from all that shit. This is supposed to be a vacation."

They lay there quietly staring at the ceiling and munching on truffles. Victoria's concerns about the book are making him paranoid. If they check him out they will learn that he has been critical in his column about Italy's involvement with the invasion of Iraq. He tries to remember if he wrote anything in his journal he might regret.

Before long he notices she has fallen asleep. But he feels too nervous to do likewise. This whole situation is just way too strange. And, he can't stop wondering what happened to Ted. The champagne is making him drowsy though and begins to doze when he and Victoria are jolted awake by an early-morning phone call. Victoria answers.

"Yes, I'd like that," she says. "I'll be ready in ten minutes."

She hangs up the phone and jumps out of bed.

"Where ya goin'?" asks Chris.

"It's Sunday and they're having mass in the chapel."

"You're going to mass?"

"When the phone rang I was having the strangest dream," she says.

"What about?"

"I can't remember but it was wonderful."

"And now you're going to church."

"Is there something wrong with that?"

"No," he says. "You just haven't gone to mass in years."

"Maybe it's all the churches we've been touring or the visit to the Vatican," she says. "I don't know. I just feel like it's the right thing to do. I want to go to confession and take communion."

"It's your immortal soul," he kids. "But, watch what you say in the confessional. The priest might be wearing a wire."

"You don't want to come?" she says.

He looks at her and grins. "If you weren't such a freak this would be weirding me out."

"Is that a no?"

"Yes."

"Yes, you want to go? Or, yes you don't?"

"No," he says. "I'm not going. I'm not spiritually hungry enough for a Eucharist breakfast."

"Fine," she says kissing him on the head. "But, I don't think they have take-out."

He rolls to the end of the bed so he can watch her get ready.

"Besides, someone should stay in the room in case they come back to pillage our stuff again."

His half-drunk, sleep-deprived brain tries to wrestle with its disjointed thoughts and emotions. He wonders if it is wise for Victoria and him to separate. Maybe he should go with her. There is a knock on the door.

Victoria leans over and kisses him. "I bet all this will be cleared up by the time I get back."

"I hope you're right," he says.

She exits the room and as the door closes behind her a panic sets in. He soars to the door. It's locked.

He is startled by the phone ringing once more. It is the investigators. They want to talk with him again. He is both reluctant and eager to tell them his suspicions about Ted.

The observation deck is deserted except for Captain Della Scalla who is seated at a table with a laptop.

"*Bon journo*, Mr. Mitchum," he says. "Please, have a seat."

Chris sits down as a waiter pours him a coffee and a glass of water.

"Have you eaten breakfast?" asks the captain.

"No, I'm fine thanks," says Chris. "I'm eager, you know, to get this over with."

"As you wish," says the captain focusing on the laptop screen.

"I think I know what this is all about. and I think I know who you are looking for," says Chris. "One of the passengers, Ted Arnold…"

The captain cuts him off. "You never told us about your criminal record."

"I was never asked. I never thought," he utters. "That was over twenty-five years ago. I was a kid."

"You called in a bomb threat at your school," says Della Scalla.

"There was no bomb. It was a stupid Halloween prank that got out of control."

"You're a man with a lot of secrets. Is there anything else?"

"Like I was about to tell you," stresses Chris. "I think I have information that might help your investigation."

"Why didn't you go to mass with your fiancée?"

"Pardon," says Chris?

"Are you an atheist?"

"Look, I'm not a terrorist. I'm a journalist. I'm one of the good guys."

"Who said anything about terrorists?"

Chris is lost for words. "I just thought."

Della Scalla continues. "You told the interrogator you were a Roman Catholic but, when you were given the opportunity to attend mass, you declined."

"That doesn't make me an atheist. Just a bad Catholic."

"Did you tell your fiancée you were going to sneak down and sabotage the bus?"

"Who told you that?"

"Please answer the question."

"It was a joke," says Chris defensively. "That's it. I want to talk to a lawyer."

"Why do you think you need a lawyer?"

"I told you the guy you want to talk to is Ted Arnold. I'm not answering any more questions until I have an attorney present."

Della Scalla looks at the screen. "There is no Ted Arnold on the passenger manifest."

"Maybe that's not his real name," says Chris desperately. "He is a tall white male, mid-fifties, U.S. citizen."

The captain gives Chris a blank look.

"Check with Stefania. She will verify that a man fitting that description was on the tour."

The captain closes the laptop and signals to the guards. "I'll give you some time to think and we'll talk again."

When Chris gets back to the room he finds the cameras and books returned and neatly placed on a baggage rack. Victoria remains absent.

He hooks the video camera up to the television and runs through footage of the trip looking for any shots he may have got of Ted. Sure enough there are several shots of him. One in particular catches his attention. It is outside the perimeter wall of Sienna. Ted is well ahead of the rest of the group and talking to someone in a black Mercedes. Chris didn't notice at the time because he was concentrating on getting Victoria and the rest of the group in the shot. Ted takes a bag from the passenger side of the car then walks out of view of the camera. Roughly, a minute later he re-appears, gets in the Mercedes and it pulls away.

Chris rewinds the video and watches it again to confirm what he saw. He pauses the camera at the clearest shot of the car and zooms in. The resolution is too grainy to make out the interior but it clearly shows Ted taking the bag and walking away. When he returns he doesn't have the bag. The revelation shoots through Chris's body like a bolt of lightning.

He picks up the phone to call Captain Della Scalla but, immediately, hangs up deciding, instead, to wait and show the footage to Victoria first. That way, she can back him up. He runs through the film a couple more times before deciding to shut off the camera and wait.

With the camera turned off the television returns to a broadcast of RAI News 24. The broadcast is in Italian but Chris is able to translate enough to get the gist. A reporter is standing at the side of a road where several police and soldiers are investigating a terrorist bombing. Chris flicks around the channels for an English station. He finds the BBC and turns up the volume.

> *While no group has claimed responsibility, police sus-*
> *pect it was the work of a suicide bomber.*

The footage shows a crane dragging what little remains of a tour bus from the bottom of a deep ravine. Chris's heart nearly jumps out his throat when he recognizes the bus.

The reporter continues.

> *Few of the passengers, who were tourists from several*
> *different countries, survived. Investigators suspect the*

bomber is a Canadian journalist named Christopher Mitchum, who has been a vocal critic of the war on terror and the invasion of Iraq. He is known to be sympathetic to militant Islamic groups and an outspoken opponent of British and American foreign policies. Police received a tip from an anonymous caller just moments before the blast but it came too late to prevent the attack. Mitchum, remains in critical condition. Ironically, he is one of the few survivors. One of the victims is believed to be Mitchum's girlfriend of six years, Victoria Allegheri. Names of the other passengers are being withheld until authorities can make a positive identification and notify next of kin.

Chris's legs give out. He collapses on the floor, staring in stunned disbelief at the screen. How could this be? What kind of sick joke is this?

"Stay calm," he tells himself. "Stay calm and wait for Victoria to come back. Where the hell is she?"

This must be some kind of counter intelligence operation, he reasons. They got the tip and got the passengers off the bus then made it look as if the bus was continuing on as scheduled. They parked it in a safe location and waited for the timer or a phone call to detonate the bomb. That's why we weren't allowed to make any calls that might tip off the terrorists. They think one of the passengers is the suicide bomber. Then, they create this story for the media so the terrorists think the attack was a success.

"But, why single me out?" he wonders. "I'm not alone in my opposition to the invasion. Christ, even the pope was critical of the war."

He picks up the phone and calls down to the front desk.

"How much longer before mass is over?" he asks.

"Mass was over an hour ago," says the attendant.

"I'm looking for my fiancée Victoria Allegheri," says Chris.

"Signorina Allegheri, checked out half an hour ago," he says.

"Checked out," says Chris. "You sure?"

"Positive."

"Where did she go?"

"She left with the other passengers."

Chris notices Victoria's bags are gone and hangs up. Why would she leave without him, without even telling him or saying good-bye? He calls and arranges another meeting with Captain Della Scalla.

When he gets to the observation deck, he pounds the table and yells at the captain.

"I want to speak to a lawyer. I refuse to be framed for this bombing."

Della Scalla shrugs. "Who told you about the bombing?"

"I saw it on the fucking TV! They're saying I'm the prime suspect. I'm not the bomber."

"We know you're not the bomber," says Della Scalla.

"Then why are you holding me?"

"We're not holding you. You are still here because you refuse to confess."

"Confess to what? I'm innocent."

"No one is innocent."

"But, this whole thing is a fabrication. No one was killed. Everyone was removed from the bus before the bomb went off."

"We know when the bomb went off," says Della Scalla. "It was Saturday, May 29 at exactly 2:15 p.m."

"That's impossible," says Chris. "We checked into the hotel at 2:30."

"2:27," says Della Scalla.

"If this is some kind of plan to trick the terrorists into coming forward and claiming responsibility, that's fine. But, I will not help you frame me."

The captain leans back in his chair. "Soon, you will figure it out and then it will be too late to confess."

"I have figured it out and I'm not saying another thing until I talk to a lawyer."

"As you wish," says Della Scalla directing the guards to take Chris back to his room.

"I write for an important paper back home. A bad review could hurt Italian tourism."

"Tourism is our last concern. Besides, this isn't Italy."

Chris's mind races back over the events following his nap in the bus. "Where is Victoria?"

"She's moved on," says the captain.

"To Florence?" asks Chris.

Della Scalla squints again, but remains silent for a moment. He licks his lips then calmly forms the word. "Home."

It takes less than a second for Chris to process the response. "I want to join her. I want to confess," he confidently professes.

"To what," asks Della Scalla?

"Everything," says Chris.

"Too late. You already know."

"No! I don't know anything."

The captain directs the guards to escort Chris away.

As the guards close in Chris is desperate to convince Della Scalla of his ignorance "I want to talk to a priest. You think I know something? Go ahead ask me. Ask me anything."

"Are you lying?" asks Della Scalla.

He is unable to respond and persist with the futility. He breaks loose from his handlers and runs to the wall on the far side of the observation deck.

"There is no use in running," yells Della Scalla.

Chris looks over the edge then back at his pursuers. "I'm not going to make this easy for you," he screams as he vaults over the wall. The ground at the base of the tower rises toward him with blinding speed.

The impact wakes him up and he finds himself drenched in sweat with his heart pounding wildly. The bus is still travelling over the rolling countryside on route to Florence. It takes a moment to adjust before he sighs with relief that it was all a dream and that Victoria is cuddled under his arm still fast asleep. His notebook has slipped from his hand and fallen to the floor. He squeezes out from behind her and picks it up then stands up and opens the overhead baggage compartment. He pulls a large bottle of water from his travel bag and chugs down half a litre. When he opens the bag to put the bottle back he finds a cell phone. It isn't his and he doesn't remember Victoria buying a new phone. He looks around at the sleeping passengers and notices Ted Arnold is not on the bus. He sets the cell phone down and quietly works his way up to Arnold's seat. Careful not to arouse suspicion from his slumbering, fellow passengers he opens the baggage compartment over Arnold's seat. Inside is a black bag. Just like the one in the video from his dream. An envelope tucked into a pouch on the side of the bag catches his attention. It is addressed to *The New York Times*.

The bus passes a sign Canto Dodici Hotel. Chris checks his watch. It is 2:14.

Caught up in his strange déjà vu he doesn't notice that Victoria has woken up and is looking for the water.

"Whose phone is this?" she asks.

Chris spins around. "No!"

There is a blinding white light followed by a deafening silence.

The darkened room is slowly illuminated by the glow of a television newscast.

Colleagues are puzzled by the actions of this veteran journalist. Publisher Linda Kruger told reporters that Chris Mitchum showed no signs of radicalization, but that he had been under a lot of stress and the trip to Italy was meant to be a working vacation to give him a break from the newsroom.

Investigators say, the phone used to detonate the bomb was purchased by Mitchum in Rome. A letter found in the wreckage allegedly written by Mitchum and addressed to The New York Times *takes responsibility for the suicide bombing and condemns the Italian government for supporting the U.S. invasion of Iraq. It is interesting that Mitchum describes the bombing as an act of 'militant self-immolation.' The same term was used in a column he published two months ago.*

Chris holds up the remote and hits pause then rewind. He stares blankly at the screen as the images scroll back and he queues the tape to the beginning again.

He can't decide if he is dreaming or if this whole experience is the biological process of his brain dying – his life flashing before his eyes like some tired cliché.

He's lost all sense of time and wonders how long he has been lying in the dark watching and rewinding the tape.

There is a knock on the door. He crawls from the bed and walks across the room just as someone slips an envelope under the door. He glances through the peephole but the hallway is empty.

Inside the envelope, he finds an assignment sheet just like the ones he used to get when he first started working as a reporter.

A hand-written sticky note is attached to the front.

> *Chris: You have dedicated your life to unravelling the contradictions between established facts and accepted truths. As a result of your work you have come to recognize the power of belief and the limitations of faith – the corruption of power and the fragility of justice.*
>
> *You were working on a story before all this happened and we think it only fair that you be given time to complete it.*
>
> *You clearly have your own views and opinions about what has happened to you but we ask that you adhere to your journalistic ethics and only write only what you know to be true.*
>
> *The finished article will be forwarded to the managing editor for consideration.*

Chris pulls out his notebook and flips to his last entry.
He reads the last sentence he wrote out loud.

> *By 2 p.m. most of the others, including my girlfriend Victoria, who is nestled comfortably under my arm, are exhausted and asleep.*

He pops the lid off his pen and writes at the bottom of the page.

Michael Troy Bridgeman became a regular *Mercury* contributor in 1991 while completing a college internship. Most of his early work for the *Mercury* was as a freelance columnist and reporter but he was a frequent fill-in for vacationing staff reporters for years. In the late 90s, the freelance opportunities dried up and he took an involuntary hiatus from journalism. He continued writing, however, and secured a series development deal with CanWest Global. The series was about an award-winning newspaper reporter whose paper is bought by a British tabloid and he is forced to write about celebrity culture and supernatural phenomenon. It was rife with social commentary about pop culture, fake news and the commercialization of mainstream media. Perhaps that's why the series was never picked up for production.

To "pay the bills" he worked as a transformer coil winder for Hammond Power Solutions and ABB in Guelph. When ABB closed, in 2005, he returned to college to study broadcast journalism. Upon graduating, he worked as a reporter and anchor for the news magazine *First Local* on Rogers TV. He also resumed freelancing work with the *Mercury* again. He wrote a weekly opinion column as well as a weekly entrepreneur profile. He did a stint as editor of *My Guelph* magazine, wrote profiles for the paper's 40-Under-40 series and produced videos for the *Mercury* website. Shortly after the *Mercury* closed he started freelancing for the online news service *Guelph Today*.

Breaking

Magda Konieczna

Curtain rises.

Stage contains long, draftsman-like table, covered in keyboards, screens, computers, and other electronics. The room is dingy, and a muddy light comes in through one small window. A bare bulb hangs from the ceiling. Computer speakers are blaring loud, angry music, probably German hip hop. Spotlight is trained on the teenager on stage. He's sitting on a greasy old desk chair. One of the wheels is missing and a piece of wood is holding it up.

TEENAGER, speaking with Eastern European accent: It's not like it's my fault or anything. I mean, I didn't tell them who to vote for. And the stories were obviously fake. If they believe them, that's their own fault. They got what they deserved.

Pause as he tap-tap-taps at the keyboard and clicks around with the mouse.

TEENAGER: Sixty-thousand American dollars.

His breath catches.

TEENAGER: Sixty-thousand American dollars.

Tap-tap-tap. He looks at the screen in disbelief.

TEENAGER: Th-th-three and a half million denars. In six months. More than my parents will make in their lifetimes.

Long pause. Angry German hip hop crescendos.

TEENAGER: I mean, if you can't live the American dream, what good is capitalism?

Pause.

TEENAGER: It started out innocently enough. And really, you can't argue that it wasn't a brilliant idea. They used to say that the internet was going to make the world more democratic, that people would engage in conversation. That we'd learn about each other.

Laughs.

TEENAGER: At least, I think that's what they used to say. Back in the 90s. Well it's not my fault I proved them wrong.

Pause.

TEENAGER: I mean, all I did was post a single story. I tweaked it. Then, I tweaked it again. And suddenly, the clicks came rolling in, like a giant wave on the Mediterranean. And then they all copied me! Two-hundred, three-hundred others. My friends. Well, one-time friends. Pause. It's not like the gold mine dried up though. That's the crazy thing. The money just kept rolling in, even as the number of sites doubled, tripled. Americans' desire for this stuff was endless!

Chortles. Tap-tap-tap. Reads off the screen.

TEENAGER: 'Do You Consider Donald Trump to be the Jesus of America?' Ha! That one was brilliant. 'BREAKING: Obama Confirms Refusal to Leave White House, He Will Stay in Power!' The most-read news articles are usually the ones containing the click-bait words. 'Oh my God, breaking news, wow.' Because if the title just says, 'Today this happened, today that happened,' no one will open that.

Picks up a newspaper lying on one of the tables.

TEENAGER, reading: 'Three hurt when car hits cow.' Yaaaawn.

Pause.

TEENAGER: And they're wondering why the mainstream news is dying.

Shakes his head.

TEENAGER: I mean, seriously. They're all high-paid executives. They went to the American universities. They worked their way up the ladder. And what? What?? Some kid in tiny Veles, some teenager with no future, with a $100 computer, can outsmart them? Of course they blame me. Of course they do.

Tap tap tap.

TEENAGER: And listen to what they say about Veles, anyway (puts on a mock serious voice): 'Visitors are greeted by a distressed

112

mosaic of red-roofed buildings…Industrial smokestacks add to a wintry fog – ooh, poetic – settling over the valley, though even their output has diminished after several recent factory closures. Almost a quarter of Macedonians are currently unemployed – a rate around five times higher than in the U.S.'

Pause.

TEENAGER: Oh, oh! They call us a 'global hotbed for fake news'!!

Beams.

TEENAGER: That's me!!! A global hotbed.

Pause.

TEENAGER: Mmmm. What's a hotbed?

Pause.

TEENAGER: NBC makes us sound like some shithole. I've never been to the U.S., but I have watched *The Wire*. I mean, at least we're not Baltimore! Anyway, it's not my fault they're so dumb.

Tap-tap-tap.

TEENAGER: 'Pope Francis forbids Catholics from Voting for Hilary!'

Smug smile.

TEENAGER: That was one of my best-sellers. See, I even tried spelling Hillary wrong. Makes no difference. They want to believe this so bad, they'll read anything.

TEENAGER: Thing is, they had it good for so long. We had Communism. We weren't Russia, but we certainly weren't on the right side of the Cold War, either. My parents had poverty, misery.

Pause.

TEENAGER: Of course, I remember none of that. Still, it's the legacy we live with. And here we are, making millions. Millions!

Pause.

TEENAGER: Well, millions of denars, at least.

TEENAGER: Meantime, what did they have? Post-war prosperity. The New Deal. Suburbanization. Unionized jobs in the car factories. The Beatles! They had the Beatles!

Pause.

TEENAGER: Wait, maybe not the Beatles. They were British, right? Well, they had Michael Jackson. Whitney Houston! Ella and Louis! And look what they did. Squandered it all.

Shakes head.

TEENAGER: What a fucked up place.

Tap-tap-tap.

TEENAGER: They say little Veles produced 140 fake news web-sites. 140!

Pause.

TEENAGER: I mean, they're just jealous. They can't believe we're better at capitalism than they are.

Pause.

TEENAGER: It's not like I *care* about Donald Trump. That guy?? Ha!

Tap-tap-tap.

TEENAGER: Look at him! That hair! That smug expression. The way he holds his head to make his chin look better.

Pause.

TEENAGER: See, my grandma knew something about that. You can tell not to trust him because he's just trying to look good for the cameras.

Pause.

TEENAGER: It's just a natural outcome. Their civilization is over. All they have left to do is sit in front of their computers, letting social media pollute their brains with garbage. Maybe I'm just helping that happen a little faster, is all. I mean, that's good for the rest of the world, isn't it?

Pause.

TEENAGER: Least, I think it is.

Pause.

TEENAGER: Yes, the info in the blogs is bad, false, and misleading, but if it gets the people to click on it and engage, then use it.

Pause.

TEENAGER: The Buzzfeed guys were pretty good, though. They tracked us down. I remember when they came knocking on my door. And then NBC. NBC! I always dreamed of being on the news.

TEENAGER: They say our work is aggregated or plagiarized. But who cares! What about their First Amendment? It protects everything. You can say anything! It used to not be that way. 'Don't yell fire in a full theatre,' and all that. Well, times have changed. They've decided they want to say anything, do anything. Carry guns. Ban people from healthcare, schools. And now they have what they deserve, right?

TEENAGER: It's not like this took no work. Nooooo. I worked twelve, fourteen hours a day. Starting with news about Democrats. What was that guy's name, the old grandpa? Saaaanders? Anyway, that didn't stick. This one was brilliant:...

Tap-tap-tap.

TEENAGER: 'Hillary Clinton in 2013: I Would Like to See People Like Donald Trump Run for Office; They're Honest and Can't be Bought.'

Tap-tap-tap.

TEENAGER: There were over 480,000 shares and Facebook comments on that one. 480,000!

Shakes head.

TEENAGER: I mean, how can that even be? I read somewhere that that big New York Times story, the one they thought would swing the election, had 175,000. Ha! Two times, three times more. The thing is, I'm giving them what they want. And they love it. They eat it up!

Shakes head.

TEENAGER: Those poor editors, with all their degrees and their Pulitzers. It's over. The time of the Pulitzer is over. Ha!

Pause.

TEENAGER: Well, it's all done now. The denars have stopped rolling in. My fake news story about Paul Ryan got a couple thousand hits. Even though I added a panda bear and a kitten!

Tap-tap-tap.

TEENAGER: Yep, 4,000. Yeesh!

Pause.

TEENAGER: Now what will I do? I haven't done my homework in weeks. Teacher seems not to care, but I can't do this forever.

Sigh.

TEENAGER: Thing is, this temporary fame thing, it's exhausting. I'm burned out!

Pause.

TEENAGER: All the naps in the world can't cure this…this emptiness. From NBC interviews, to Veles. Sigh.

TEENAGER: What did the article say again? Distressed buildings…industrial smokestacks…wintry fog…output has diminished… almost a quarter unemployed –

Pause.

TEENAGER: It's true. What a shithole. Welllll…I guess I should spend some of my millions. That's not a bad idea, right? Maybe I'll go on a little vacation by the sea. Get that cabin we stayed in years ago. This time, I'll be able to rent the whole place! Won't have to share it with the mothers and loud kids running around! Maybe I'll get the owner to still come cook for me though…

Pause.

TEENAGER: And then? What is there to return here for? A quarter of us are unemployed. We are famous for lying about American politics. We have distressed red roofs and diminished output.

Sigh. Puts his head on the table. German hip hop has died down. Clock ticks.

TEENAGER, lifts head, brightens: Well, there must be an election going on somewhere, right?

Tap tap tap.

TEENAGER: Hm. General municipal election in Missouri. What does that mean?

Tap tap tap.

TEENAGER: Wait a second…French presidential election, April 23.

Pause.

TEENAGER: St. George's day. I wonder if that's a good sign, or bad?

Tap tap tap.

TEENAGER: Oy, this woman, what's her name? Le Pen. Ugh, she's quite terrible. 'Marine Le Pen: Impossible made possible by Trump win.'

Pause, as he reads:

TEENAGER: 'No place for multiculturalism…a prominent Euroskeptic…attempting to "detoxify" the party somewhat of its reputation for racism and xenophobia, focusing instead on anti-EU and anti-immigration policies…'

Shakes head.

TEENAGER: What is this world coming to? What?? First Brexit, now Trump, then Le Pen? How will Macedonia ever enter the West if the West is busy killing itself to get out some people who don't look like them??

Pause.

TEENAGER: So disgusting.

Pause.

TEENAGER: Seriously. Grownups are terrible.

Pause.

TEENAGER: Hm. Where do I fit in to all of this, I wonder?

Pause.

TEENAGER: I mean, if there's money to be made, I should make it. Right?

Pause.

TEENAGER, scratching his head: Like, it really would be dumb not to. There's money, free for the taking. Right?

Pause.

TEENAGER: Whatever happens isn't my responsibility. Right?

Pause. German hip hop crescendos, dies down. Lights begin to dim.

TEENAGER: Right??

———————————

Magda Konieczna was an intern, reporter and copy editor at the *Guelph Mercury* from 2006 to 2009, a job, and a place, she still misses every single day. She's now a journalism professor at Temple University, in Philadelphia, where she's working on a book about the news business.

The Errand

Drew Halfnight

To be struck or clipped, thrown and killed while bicycling on the side of a large boulevard would make for a pathetic end. Really it was a small highway. *Ffffewh, ffffewh, ffffewh,* the cars exhaled, making a sharp, shooting sound as they passed. When the vehicles came closer, Rose could feel a distinct sideways yank toward the traffic, as if her bike had a death wish.

Rose considered the situation. Somewhere east of Mimico, the map had flown off the back of the bike. She had wrapped it in a plastic bag and tucked it under a bungee cord with her fleece on the rear rack. The bike had rattled pretty hard over potholes and faults in the pavement and also swayed somewhat in the gusts from off the lake. The map had become dislodged.

Fuck it, she thought, trying to imagine something positive that might arise from an obvious handicap. Maybe getting a little lost would lead to adventure, surprises, a happy ending. The idea that an instance of loss could be reframed as a net gain was ludicrous, of course, but also comforting and appealing in its counter-intuitiveness, like talk-show mantra. *With adversity comes…No pain…Freedom is letting go…Bad things happen to good people. Life is what you make of it.* And there was that line from a poem about how losing ain't no disaster.

> *Tomorrow at dawn, when the countryside whitens,*
> *will leave. You see, I know you are expecting me.*

There was nothing to do but continue. The route from Toronto to the border hugged the shoreline all the way. If Rose stuck on her path between the eight lanes of the Queen Elizabeth Way and Lake Ontario, she could not get lost.

Now a spectral sun was rising over downtown, tinting the sky with amber and frosting the buildings and beaches with white. Then there was blue overhead, thin air, a minor breeze. Rose was glad she had packed light, only allowing herself the fleece, a toque, a pair of leggings in case of cold or rain. The scenery passed like a moving picture. She stopped to take photos of a factory silhouetted against the sun in Mississauga, a Canada goose padding down a dead-end street in Oakville.

Rose sat upright on the narrow seat and steadied herself. She used her right hand to pull sunglasses from the zippered breast pocket of her windbreaker. It was only 10 a.m. but her lower back had begun to ache. She had slept poorly the night before, tormented by the vivid scenes she imagined unfolding when she reached her destination. Michael always cast her penchant for daydreaming and fantasy in a positive light. He would have appreciated her impulse this time. This was a journey to cast herself at the feet of her beloved. She would lay bare her feelings for the angels to witness and judge. She hoped for mercy. She prayed for reconciliation. She closed her eyes against doubt, even as its shadow pursued her.

I will go through the forests, I will go by the mountain.
I cannot stay away from you any longer.

Now she was pedaling hard, eyes fixed on the asphalt path, and the bike was keeping time with its *klik, klik ka-lik, klik-ka-dlik, klik.* Rose's mountain bike, spray-painted black, was a little too small, forcing her to ride high and forward. She had bought it from a repairman in Kensington Market who advertised on Craigslist. "Are you sure it isn't a kid's bike?" she asked him when they met on the street in front of the shop. Her toes shot up an inch too high on each pedalling cycle. Her knees were complaining. She thought again of Michael. The temptation to weep stabbed suddenly between her cheat and her throat. Rose supressed it.

The Errand

Later, passing under the drawbridge at Hamilton Harbour, Rose felt some of the weight she had carried during the winter loosen and fall away. What a gift, this coordinating her limbs to convey her body swiftly over the ground, locomoting for miles at a time, she thought. An absurd vision of her body's exertions formed in her mind. Legs pulsing, hips wagging, head bobbing, hands flexing over the rubber grips, a crude cartoon from the 1960s played on in her brain for a few seconds. A series of belts and pipes carried a bright red liquid – blood, love, the fuel – from the heart to the limbs. She inhaled fiercely, crinkling her nose, unleashed a growl that nobody heard.

I will walk with my eyes fixed on my thoughts,
Not seeing anything outside, not hearing any noise,
Alone, unknown, back bent, hands crossed,
Sad, and the day for me will be like the night.

Scraps of a poem entered and left her head. Since childhood, she had the habit of memorizing verse. She recited Lewis Carroll and Edward Lear at a school assembly, swooned to Dylan Thomas in high school, made Prufrock her party trick in university. Now, whenever she walked alone or waited for the bus in the cold, the poems kept her company. She recited them under her breath, and they comforted her. Michael often asked her to send him a poem, and once in a while they resurfaced in his letters and cards, even in the speeches he wrote for work.

Despite the high, the enduring buzz, of what she had felt from the first time she met Michael – on her doorstep, in shadow and light – in the sixteen years she had known him, she had never given in to her feelings, and to the extent he felt the same longing, he had not either. Once, drying off after a storm, they lay on Michael's bed and somehow ended up holding hands. Her body went completely numb before he pulled his hand away, in glee, in terror, from boredom, because he was hungry and wanted to fix a snack. It was impossible to know. Another time, at a bar in Peterborough, on New Year's Eve, he kissed her and hugged her aggressively, mumbled and shouted something unusually affectionate. Was this his *in vino veritas* moment? Had he mustered the courage to come on to her? The memory faded in a fog of drink and smoke.

After the accident in the fall, her crush matured and became conviction. She had always loved him. She had never stopped loving him. She had always had the habit of thinking about him when they were separated. Now those same thoughts kept pace with her progress over the ride. She imagined his simple face, his far-away eyes, his delicate body. She listened for his peculiar inflection. "You are such a good person," she heard him say. In her mind he knew her worst fear, that somehow she was not good. That in a world of war and murder, of bad things, we were all evil's hapless accomplices.

> *I will not look at the gold evening falling,*
> *Nor at the far off boats sailing towards Harfleur,*

Before noon, Rose discovered Grimsby Beach, a neighbourhood of multicoloured gingerbread heritage homes where a man named Ed took a break from painting to explain the history of the town. "This scrollwork trim you see on all the houses, a lot of that is from the original Victorian construction. The rest I've put on myself," he said. "As for the cha-cha colours, that's all me." He invited the young rider from Toronto in for tea – people rarely stopped here – but she had to get moving, she said, begging off.

In Port Dalhousie, a glass condominium towered over red-brick storefronts. She parked her bike in front of a cafe and ordered a bowl of soup. On a television mounted overhead, a reporter with mannequin cheekbones delivered the news of the day: typhoid among Syrians detained at Calais, Donald Trump at the inauguration of a golf course in Scotland. "They took back control of their country," Trump said, his familiar features popping against a yellow lodge in the background. From a distance, Rose heard the highway's droning din seep through the air.

Rose knew she had arrived in Niagara when pink and gray subdivisions yielded to brown and gray vineyards. In the middle of one vineyard, an 18-wheel transport truck lay with a 'for sale' sign on the dash. A tall, blue wildflower cluster lined the ditch. It was a pretty colour Rose had noticed all summer. She pulled a bunch and wrapped them up carefully in her fleece and fastened them where the map had been.

The cemetery on Lakeshore Road was impossible to miss. Rose turned onto a paved, black lane threading two stately trees. She passed a long, high hedge and entered a wilderness of oaks and maples sheltering groves of headstones, which she read as she rolled along, Armstrong, Lester…Chung, Davis, Borden. Within the hedges, far from the road, the sounds of the cities and highways receded. Rose's bike clicked and whined in the silence. Images of dead bodies arose unbidden in her mind: first she saw them prostrate under the plots, then she remembered her grandfather in the old churchyard in Etobicoke, and then her cousin, her classmate Allan who committed suicide. She braked, took a swig of water from her bottle, reviewed the scribbled notes in her journal. "Plot 47971 / End of main road / On right / MJR / Safe in the Arms of the Earth." Deeper and deeper she rode, until she was descending into a gully at what felt like the heart or the bottom of the cemetery.

Rounding a row of mausoleums, Rose came suddenly upon a tall figure stooping by a grave. On the headstone where the figure stood, the name REVERE was blazoned in solemn script, though in this strange city of gray slabs, Rose barely recognized Michael's surname. And who was this woman? – for now she could make out the figure's fine features and shapely head. In her long, black overcoat and high collar, she resembled a pallbearer. Yet she had a certain appeal, Rose could see, with her chestnut hair pulled up in a messy, rakish bun and fastened with red bobby pins. She was placing some token on Michael's grave.

Rose tried to make sense of this unexpected intrusion from her bicycle idyll. She coasted past the grave, braked, circled back, dismounted, lay her bike on the grass, and stepped forward. "Hello," she said, chopping her hand sideways in a timid wave.

The woman did not seem to hear her. Rose was gathering her breath to hail her again when finally she turned her head and looked Rose in the eyes, smiling mildly. She introduced herself as Jessica, asked if Rose were also visiting Michael, and had she attended the memorial, and how had she known him?

"Well, we were old friends, more than friends really; he and I used

122

to hang out all the time, back in university, and afterward. We were sort of soulmates," Rose said, trying to satisfy this stranger's curiosity with some sort of story. "I haven't seen him as much since he moved to Niagara," she went on. "I never really got the chance to say goodbye."

The woman listened, smiling and nodding politely, though Rose wondered if she detected a hint of forbearance in her expression, some condescension around the eyes, as if she were the one intruding on this woman's, this Jessica's, errand. Now, it was Rose's turn for questions.

As she answered, Jessica arranged flowers on the grave, and Rose noticed they were peonies, a large bunch, fresh and pretty, probably expensive. "Michael and I both worked in politics," she said. "We met several years ago. He was an assistant in St. Catharine's; I was an assistant in Niagara Falls. We only became close in the last few years. Michael had more passion for the work than anyone I know. His heart was in it, you know?"

She managed to say all this as if Rose didn't know what Michael did for a living, or that he had been a policy wonk all his life, or that he had spent the last ten years as a constituency assistant."

"Michael taught me how to really love," the woman was saying. "We travelled to Argentina together last summer…" Then she took her face in her hands and, weeping openly (and a little dramatically, Rose thought), allowed her grief to take centre stage for what must have been a full two minutes. All the while, Michael's headstone towered between them, a mute witness to their encounter.

Rose examined the thing. It was a simple ashen tablet with none of the crosses, statues, or other embellishments she had seen on other markers. Standing almost as high as Rose's shoulders, it was festooned with flowers, some of which exuded a powerful fragrance she found somehow both sweet and repulsive. A rectangle of fresh dirt heaved in front of the grave. Rose had intended to put a few keepsakes there: a bicycle bell and a picture. But now she was distracted by doubts. Should she console this woman? Touch her back? When Jessica's sobbing finally ebbed, the woman did not apologize, but just stared off, away from Rose, away from the cemetery, away from her grief presumably.

They both stood silently by Michael's resting place for a long while. The woman showed no sign of leaving, so finally, a little tired, a little bored, Rose went to her bike, withdrew the wildflowers from the rack, placed them on the grave, improvising in her mind a silent prayer for Michael's spirit in whatever after-life might happen to exist, mounted her bike, and pedaled away.

> *And when I arrive, I will put on your grave*
> *A bunch of green holly and heather in bloom.*

By the funeral centre next to the parking lot, a procession of cars had begun arriving for a burial. The air rang with the mournful noise of car doors thudding closed and the soles of expensive shoes slapping the pavement. An aged couple, hunched in dark jackets, held onto each other as they muddled through the parking lot. Rose stopped cycling, gliding silently past to show respect for their venerable years, their mountains and moons of grief. The sun, still high, was descending, and Rose yearned suddenly for the quiet refuge of a room. She headed for the exit. The errand was done.

Starting in 2010, Drew Halfnight served the *Mercury* as a news intern for one year before returning to his native Toronto. He continued writing a twice-monthly column for the paper until 2013. During his short but fruitful stint in Guelph, Drew co-wrote a series on the state of public transit in the city and won the Ontario Newspaper Award for Novice Reporting for stories about a local firm selling Internet filtering software to repressive governments and the problem of addiction in the Canadian military. Drew now teaches English and French at an independent school in Toronto. He thanks the *Mercury* staff for their mentorship and friendship, his sources for their faith and candour, and the *Mercury* readership for their support of the paper through good times and bad.

It's Me

Brad Needham

This is not about me. This is not about me.

Brian repeated this over and over, like it was his new mantra. But if he had to keep saying it, didn't that mean it was about him? He said it to himself in his car, outside the church, in its near-empty and freshly plowed parking lot. The car was running. It's heater was cranked and directed to apply warmth to his feet. It was early, because he was early. He had taken the red-eye and rented a car from the airport. Toyota Venza. Go figure. The same car he had at home. At least it was a different colour. The windows fogged. This is not about me, he repeated again. That's the last thing Troy had ever said to him.

"It's always about you. How is this good for me? That's how you've always operated. It's why you have no friends left."

That was two years ago. He wrote it on Facebook. He didn't actually say it. It happened right after Brian found out that Troy had terminal cancer. Before that, they had a little communication, commenting on each other's Facebook photos, but they hadn't actually spoken for years. Fifteen years ago, Troy was his best man. What happened? Life happened, right?

"You reach out now that I'm sick? Why, to be the hero?" Sitting in his rental, with the snow falling, those words rung through Brian's head. I'm no goddamned hero, he thought. But it still pissed him off to remember.

Now, in the church parking lot, Brian wondered if he should go to the funeral. Forty-two years old and he was still worried about what people would think, like a teenager going into a school dance. He was invited. Terry, Troy's wife, had invited him. Brian was sure Troy wouldn't want him there. Why would he? When Brian tried to reach out, Troy flatly rejected him. Blocked him from Facebook. It was a slap. He hadn't just unfriended him, he had blocked him. And Brian just gave up. How can I contact him now, he thought? I can't even apologize, he thought. Not that he wanted to. Or thought he had to. All about me? What about you, Troy?, he thought.

＊＊＊＊＊

"Eight ball, corner pocket," Steve said.

It was a night of revelry. In their earlier teens every Friday night was. Saturday night too. And, sometimes, Sunday night as well. Now, they had all either just left their teens behind or soon would. And, Brian and Troy had started to drift apart. Brian felt like he should make time for Troy. Until Brian started university, Brian, Troy, Matt and Steve went out almost every Friday night. In the past year, that changed. Brian had new friends. But tonight, in the smoky pool hall – pool hall and bowling alley, to be exact, down the stairs and under the IGA – they were a few drinks in and it was just like old times.

Brian was the designated driver. Like that was actually a thing. He would have drank even less, but Troy kept refilling his glass while Matt and Steve bumbled through a game of eight ball. The more they drank, the more apparent their lack of expertise became but the less they cared. And their clumsy play provided Brian and Troy more time to fill and drink and fill and drink. Alas, the pool hall was never the final stop. Just an early warm-up for the night ahead.

Steve made his shot, just as called, or mostly. Eight ball in the corner pocket, followed by the cue ball in the side pocket. It was go-time. Steve and Matt downed what was left in their glasses, and off they went.

"Shotgun!" Troy said, as the reached the top of the dirty staircase. It reeked of urine, though that might have been because all of them urinated halfway up, before tipsily bounding up the last dozen stairs to the parking lot.

Brian was driving his old Sunbird. It wasn't much to look at but it was a six-cylinder with more horses than you'd expect. And the exhaust hung low, so as they sped through the city, sparks would fly with every bump. It was the perfect street-racing car. Well, they didn't call it street-racing back then. That sounded so illegal. Just racing. But his unassuming, rusting grey car could really move, especially off the line. And move it did. Many surprised would-be racers were left in its dust.

The light was red. It had just started to drizzle when the Viper pulled up beside them and its driver revved its engine, the sound of raw American engine-power filling the air. Troy, pushing harder than usual, egged Brian on. "Don't be a pansy," he slurred, the effects of the drinks taking full hold. Not one to decline a challenge, Brian revved, knowing full well he couldn't win. But, a few drinks in, some egging on and a perfect opportunity – you've got to take it, right? If only to see what four hundred horses could really do. The other driver looked over and smiled.

"Just gun it right before the light turns green. Get a head start. It's a Viper, for fuck's sake," Troy said, laughing. "He owes you at least that much." And then there was a strange moment of peace. The four of them, laughing and joking, like a scene out of *Stand by Me*, just older and drunker. Matt and Steve adding to the light-hearted, alcohol-induced taunting from the back seat. When had they last been this happy?

"Go, go, go," Troy shouted, breaking the peace. And Brian did. While it's not all clear, he has little bits of detail of what happened etched into his mind. He hammered the gas, the wheels squealed on the freshly wet pavement, delaying the inevitable for a split second, and then they surged into the intersection. The car was T-boned. It was struck on the passenger-side fender, just before the door, and Troy was tossed like a ragdoll against the side door and window. It shattered in slow motion, at least in Brian's memory. The car spun around and hit the light standard. They were taken to the hospital. Brian, Matt and Steve had minor injuries, but Troy was in bad shape. Brian was told Troy hadn't been wearing his seatbelt. On top of a DUI, a lost licence and some broken ribs, Brian also had to live with the guilt. Troy suffered a serious head injury, broken bones – including his right femur – and some internal bleeding.

For a few years after, he and Troy were closer again, even though

Troy was not the same. The head injury changed him. He stopped drinking and it was easier than ever to piss him off. But on the bright side, he met Terry. And, within months or so it seemed to Brian, Troy and Terry were married. He and Troy started seeing less and less of each other once Terry entered the picture. In his last year of university, Brian spent more time with his new crew, and much less with Troy. Troy still made Brian his best man. More guilt.

In two years, Troy and Terry had two kids. Brian wasn't even close to settled like that. But, then, Brian met Karen. Three years later, they married. While Brian and Troy rarely spoke, he asked Troy to be his best man. It seemed like the right thing to do. The next year, Brian got a job and moved across the country. He tried to keep in touch with Troy. He always felt responsible for him.

Only years later did Brian learn Troy had unbuckled his seatbelt at the intersection – while the Viper was revving its engine. Troy had told Matt a couple of years after the crash that he released the belt as he took in the traffic lights and saw another vehicle approaching, an oncoming F-150. Then, he'd shouted "Go!" Apparently he was depressed. Trying to kill himself – without having to do it himself. So much for that moment of peace and happiness Brian remembered. For years Brian wore the guilt of the accident. And Brian was selfish?

* * * * *

Yes. Yes, he was. He was selfish. He must be. If he thought about himself now, when he was trying not to, how much did he think about himself when he wasn't? OK, he'd go in. But a church? Troy wasn't religious when he was younger but he'd found God after he got married. Brian turned off the car. OK, he muttered to himself. Let's go.

* * * * *

Once friends for fifteen years. Now, friends fifteen years ago. What had happened?

The memories of the best times came in a sudden torrent. The epic Pacific Coast road trip where his old VW bug sputtered-out and died every four or five hours, like a tired, old horse in need of a drink and some shade. More than 4,000 kilometres! They had to stop to let it cool. Or, the time when they went snowboarding, way out of bounds, on an especially snowy day. The next day there was an avalanche in the same area and three people were killed. Brian felt lucky to be alive that day. Did Troy? Maybe he was cursing himself or Brian for their impeccable – or atrocious – timing.

They had spent so much time together as kids. Almost every weekend during the summers. For years. Playing guns – when toy guns looked real and you could play with them in the streets without fear of actually being shot. They were just kids being kids. Trips to the mall just for the sake of being at the mall. Shoplifting crappy CDs. Was it called Rap Tracks? No, Rap Traxx, with X's for effect. Brian was two years older than Troy, so there were a few summers when the gap between their interests seemed to turn into a vast chasm – GI Joe or party line? But they got through it. They always did. Or mostly. University was the great divide for them. Brian met new friends. But he still loved Troy like a brother, didn't he? He just didn't want to hang out as much. So, did he love him like a brother? If he did, wouldn't he have made more of an effort to stay in touch? Wouldn't he have tried to reach out, again, even after being told he was a selfish asshole when he knew his friend was dying?

* * * * *

He sat in his car for another fifteen minutes after he shut it off. The blue Venza was a far cry from his old Sunbird. Even when he rented a car, he rented a practical family car. Cars were no longer for racing, looking cool or driving friends around. For many years now, they were for driving his young kids to hockey practice, for grocery shopping outings, for family trips to the cottage. Troy's kids were now teenagers. Well, the two Brian knew were teens. Two were a little younger. He'd only met the elder two a couple of times. He'd seen pictures of the younger ones on Facebook. Before Brian was blocked. He should have been Uncle Brian. Now what would he be? Brian the Betrayer. Brian my douche bag former friend. Brian why the hell are you at my funeral? If Troy could talk, that's probably what he'd be asking right now.

Other cars had started to arrive, and everyone else promptly exited their cars. Solemn- looking, or from what he could tell through his foggy windows. Once the fog cleared – both literal and figurative – he would see all these old familiar faces again, and many he'd never met because he was an absent friend for the past fifteen years. What had Troy said to them about him? Maybe nothing. Nothing at all. Is that worse? They had probably all stayed in touch. But Brian moved away. He had a new job and a wife. Troy had kids. And they lost touch. It happens, right?

* * * * *

He opened his door slowly. I can do this, he said. I still love him. He was like a brother, Brian thought. Why did I let it get to this point? He walked toward the door of the church. When he grabbed its big handle and pulled, seemingly taking everything he had in him to do it, he met Terry's gaze. He paused for second, but continued. He had to go.

"Brian," Terry said kindly, sadly. "Troy would've been so happy to know you came. You were like a brother to him." Bullshit, Brian wanted to say, but he restrained himself.

"Really? I didn't get that impression the last time we talked," Brian said meekly. "I was worried..." he trailed off. It wasn't about him, but it felt like it was right now – as this kind woman, this woman who loved Troy so, embraced him.

"Well, a cousin at the very least," she said, with a warm half-smile.

A cousin, Brian thought. He hugged Terry again, tightly, and walked to his seat.

Brad Needham is a journalist whose career can be broken into three parts: *Guelph Mercury* and pre- and post-Mercury. Brad graduated from Mount Royal University, in Calgary, with a Bachelor of applied communications specializing in journalism, and then worked at several daily newspapers as editor and reporter/writer, first in Alberta (Fort McMurray and Red Deer) before moving to Ontario to follow the love of his life. He worked as news editor at the *Woodstock Sentinel Review* before moving on to the *Barrie Examiner* and then to the *Mercury*, in 2006, the same year he married his true love and lifelong editor, Jen.

At the *Mercury*, Brad filled various roles, from editor/designer to sometimes contentious columnist and night news editor. Two of Brad's three proudest career accomplishments came at the *Mercury*: winning an international design award from the Society for News Design (and later winning two more) and redesigning the *Mercury*. Brad also won one and was a finalist for two Ontario Newspaper Awards for design. After the *Mercury*, Brad moved on to the *Waterloo Region Record* and then *The Toronto Star*.

In 2013, weeks after his daughter, Quinn, was born, Brad moved on to Pagemasters North America, which was preparing to take on much of the production of *The Toronto Star*. Steering this team, now more than twenty talented editors, to success on this project is Brad's other proudest career accomplishment.

Fugitive Among Us

Scott Tracey

Todd had always hated little yappy dogs, and he now found himself hating this particular one more than most.

As the minute ginger-coloured Pomeranian yelped and once again eluded his grasp, Todd cast a glance through the windshield at the giant stomping towards him.

"Is there someone taking pictures in that van?" the Scotsman bellowed a second time, his red-bearded face growing even more deeply coloured, as he gestured at Todd with the well-used spade he clenched in his massive left fist.

Oh how he hated these little yappy dogs.

* * * * *

Todd had been sitting in the *Times'* musty newsroom a week earlier, sipping his morning coffee and perusing the lengthy agenda for the upcoming city council meeting, when his phone rang.

"Good afternoon, are you one of the journalists there?" the caller asked in a heavy Scottish accent.

The caller identified himself as Stewart Craig, a reporter with the *Glasgow Herald* newspaper. Craig had been investigating the disappearance of Colin McNally, who'd vanished approximately a year earlier in the middle of a trial on fraud charges. McNally was the key figure in a rather significant pyramid scheme, and by the time authorities closed the net more than a hundred investors had been bilked of at least three million pounds.

"It seems he used some of the proceeds and bought himself into the harness racing industry in your part of the world," Craig said. "Bought a little horse farm not too far from you."

All thoughts of municipal subdivision agreements swept from his mind, Todd had flipped open his green steno notebook and began taking notes, including the address his Scottish colleague had tracked down for the fugitive McNally.

"Fairly common name over here, so unless you knew what you were looking for it would be difficult to connect the dots," Craig said, "especially half a world away."

A day later, Todd rolled up to a cute white-and-green farmhouse with a large barn and several acres of horse corrals. As he climbed the stairs to the wrap-around porch, Todd heard a small dog barking from the enclosed backyard.

Yip, yip, yip.

Before he could knock, the wood-framed screen door was shoved open by a large man who filled the frame of the entranceway.

"Help you?" the man barked, with the tone of someone unaccustomed to – and not particularly welcoming of – visitors.

"Hello," Todd replied, pulling the green steno book from the back waistband of his jeans. "I'm looking for a Colin McNally."

"He's no' here," the man said, eyeing the notebook suspiciously. "Who's lookin' for 'im?"

Todd identified himself, handing over a business card and explaining he would like to speak to McNally about some outstanding matters back home.

Yip, yip, yip. The dog went off again. Yap, yap, yap.

"Shut yer face, Maggie!" the man bellowed in the general direction of the small dog, who declined the invitation.

"Maggie?" Todd asked.

"Aye, named for another mouthy bitch."

Todd briefly considered asking if the dog's name was intended as a political statement. And, then, quickly, thought better of it.

"Colin's no' here," the man repeated. "Travellin' in the States right now."

The man identified himself as "Mark Finnegan," the farm's manager.

"Could I get the spelling, of your name, so I can tell my editor who I spoke to?" Todd asked, pen poised over a blank page.

"M-A-R-K," he spat.

Todd wrote this down and waited for more. Then, waited some more. The dog broke the silence.

Yip. Yip. Yip. Yap. Yap.

"Yes. Thank you Mark. And, can you spell out your last name as well," Todd asked, as the latest barking blast concluded.

"F, I, N...erm...G, A, N."

"Unusual spelling," Todd said.

The large man's face clouded over. "I'll tell Colin you're looking for 'im."

Yip. Yip. Yip. Yap.

Driving back to the office, Todd couldn't help but wonder if he'd just been face to face with a fugitive.

"Farm manager my ass," he muttered.

Back in the newsroom, Todd wrote an email to Craig, detailing his visit to the farm and asking his Scottish colleague for a description of McNally. He also asked if he knew anything of a Mark 'Fingan,' pronounced 'Finnegan.'

As he sat at his desk, coming up empty on Google image searches for either Colin McNally or Mark Fingan, Todd was surprised to see the notification of an email from Craig, given it was nearly 10 p.m. in Glasgow.

"Never heard of Mark Fingan," the email read, "Odd spelling that. As for McNally, I haven't been able to locate a photo but if you can get a pic of your man Fingan I could tell you if it's really McNally...built like a small car standing on end, maybe 6'4 and nearly as wide, red hair and thick beard last I saw him. Hope that helps."

Todd thought the description closely resembled the man calling himself Mark Fingan. Pronounced Finnegan.

"Thanks for quick response," Todd typed. "Sounds like same guy. Will try to get a pic for confirmation."

The next morning Todd brought his editor up to speed, describing the meeting with Fingan and the email from Stewart Craig.

"Pretty circumstantial," his editor, Andy Philips, said. "Big men with red hair are hardly rare in Scotland, from my knowledge of the place. We need to find a photo."

Todd learned from online searches that McNally operated Oatmeal Savage Stables, the mailing address of which was the farm Todd visited a day earlier. The Stables' spartan website included generic photos of barns and several horses trotting on a track, one of them cheekily named Ponzi Scheme.

"Cocky bastard," Todd chuckled to himself, jotting the horse's name in his steno book.

He reached Byron Shortbridge, president of the provincial harness racing association, and explained he was considering a feature on Colin McNally, which was entirely true.

"Don't know much about the man," Shortbridge said. "Started hanging around the tracks towards the end of last season. Asking a lot of questions. Talking about buying some ponies. Seemed to have pretty deep pockets but limited knowledge of the horse industry."

"You wouldn't have any photos of him by chance?" Todd hoped the question didn't seem too odd, but the resulting silence suggested he had inadvertently hoisted a red flag.

"I could check with our secretary," Shortbridge said at last, suspicion evident in his voice. "But if you're doing a story on Colin why don't you just ask him for a photo?"

Why not indeed.

"I understand he's away on business at the moment, so I'm just trying to compile some background information." Todd realized as he was speaking how ridiculous he sounded.

"I think you're misinformed," Shortbridge said. "I saw him at the track a day or two ago. What's this really about?"

Fearing the horse official would spill the beans – and kicking himself for how poorly this interview had gone – Todd told Shortbridge all he thought he knew about Colin McNally.

"Well that's not good," Shortbridge said. "Not good at all. You know one of his horses is named Ponzi Scheme? When I asked him about it he said owning a horse is a good way to lose a lot of money.

"Which is true enough," he added with a nervous laugh.

They rang off with Shortbridge noting this information would necessarily require a full investigation by his agency, but promising he could keep a lid on it a few days while Todd chased his story.

The next afternoon, Todd pulled his rusty Dodge Caravan over one kilometre from McNally's farm, just long enough for the newspaper's photographer Brian Porter to slip from the front seat into the back. The plan was a simple one; Todd would approach the farmhouse and try to speak to the man who claimed to be the farm's manager. As he did so, Brian – hidden behind the Caravan's tinted rear windows – would snap photos of the suspected fugitive.

"Colin's still no' here," the large man said by way of greeting as he pushed open the screen door, stepping onto the porch and unknowingly into view of Brian's camera. Maggie followed him through the screen door, her high-pitched yelping incessant.

Yap. Yap Yap.

"Are you sure you're not him?" Todd ventured. "The descriptions I've heard of Mr. McNally sound a lot like you."

The big man sighed.

"Some people say we look alike, but I'm no' him. I'll let 'im know you came by. Again."

"Sorry, what did you say your name was?" Todd asked.

"You wrote it in your wee book the last time," the big man said, nodding towards Todd's van. "Have a nice day."

Figuring Brian had been given enough time to accomplish his task, Todd thanked the man for his time and began towards the driveway.

Maggie followed, yelping at his heels.

Yip. Yap. Yip.

"Sorry Maggie, you can't come," Todd said, forcing a laugh.

But the ginger-coloured Pomeranian had other ideas. When Todd opened the driver's door she jumped inside the van.

Todd scrambled to grab her, momentarily oblivious to the open driver's door and the illuminated interior light and to Brian, who now sat clearly exposed with the cannon-like zoom lens in his hands.

"Is there someone taking pictures in that van?" the large man yelled, pulling on an old pair of work boots.

Oh crap, Todd thought. as Maggie scurried deeper into the vehicle.

"Is there someone taking pictures in that van?" the giant bellowed a second time, closing the distance from porch to driveway in a dozen steps and tearing open the sliding side door with the hand not holding the rusty spade.

"I'll delete them!" Brian yelled, panic in his voice and eyes. "I can delete them."

Todd and the red-faced giant looked on as one by one images of the giant appeared on the camera's rear screen and then dissolved away with a press of the DEL button.

"I don't want to see either of you ever again," the Scotsman said as he scooped up his tiny dog.

Sounds good to me, Todd thought as he closed the driver's door and turned the key in the ignition.

* * * * *

Two days later Todd sat at his desk, smiling at the front page of that day's Times.

A fugitive among us? the headline posed in 72-point type, above a near-lifesize headshot of the man since positively identified as Colin McNally. Nice trick recovering the photos from the camera's deleted files folder, though Brian was taking no credit. Below the photo was simply 'Photo by Times staff.'

The accompanying article – which included Todd's byline – detailed McNally's legal troubles back home and the now-ongoing investigation by the harness racing association, which would likely see him banned from the sport. And it included his denial about his identity, and his curious spelling of a name pronounced Finnegan.

Ideas for several possible follow-up stories were already swirling through Todd's head as he left for the day, smiling and riding the familiar high of landing a big scoop.

As he crossed the parking lot, Todd became aware of a familiar sound, competing with the whir of the forklift unloading skids of advertising fliers.

As his ears focused on the high-pitched yelping, his eyes fell on the ginger-coloured fur and tartan collar next to his van.

"I hate those yappy little dogs," Todd said.

Scott Tracey joined the *Guelph Mercury* in 1991 on what was to be a six-month maternity leave coverage, and over the next twenty-two years covered most news beats, including education, health, agriculture, entertainment, courts and crime and most recently City Hall. He also wrote the weekly Jury of One column, which continued until the newspaper's closure in early 2016. During his time at the *Mercury* Scott's work was honoured with several provincial and one National Newpaper Award and a nomination for excellence in investigative journalism from the Canadian Association of Journalists. Since 2014 he has worked as a dispatcher and 911 operator for Waterloo Regional Police. Scott lives in Guelph with his wife Cathy and has three adult children aged eighteen through twenty-two.

The Move

Kathleen Elliott

Gertie hadn't been much of a mother. I knew it. She knew it. But we kept up appearances all the same. We looked just like any other family in the working-class, north-end neighbourhood where we lived. We owned a tiny, yellow, bungalow, similar to all the other little wartime houses and the six of us co-existed in roughly a thousand square feet for almost twenty years.

While other families moved, finding their way to bigger, better and newer neighbourhoods, we stayed put. I didn't think about it much at the time – and I probably couldn't have put a name to the feeling even if I had – but there was always a kind of sadness around our house when someone moved away. It wasn't just because we were losing our neighbours and playmates. There was a sense we were being left behind. I always knew such a move was coming when Gertie and Ron would fight. Normally, they didn't speak much to each other – unless we were out in public – but just before another neighbour was set to move, the yellow house at 16 Walker Lane would feel smaller than its size. The mood within its walls would change and the insults and name-calling would begin. Someone was getting out and it wasn't Ron and Gertie Miller.

But like I said, I didn't think about it much. I just went on with my life. It became normal to watch young families move in and out. Every few months it seemed there was a moving truck on the street, hauling away cardboard boxes, furniture – and memories. I learned not to get too attached to anyone. Not even my own family.

Maybe you think I wasn't a very good son or that I was a cold person. The truth is, I was as good as the role models I'd had, and in case you hadn't guessed, that's not saying much. I knew what went on inside our house wasn't normal – it hadn't been since I was about three or four – but there were spoken and unspoken rules you just accepted. No amount of hoping or just thinking about our life being different would change that. So, I spent most of my time outside, where kids didn't talk about what happened behind closed doors. Our neighbourhood was always noisy and filled with kids playing in the street. If we weren't playing ball or riding our bikes, we were goofing off – sometimes sitting down by the railroad tracks looking at dirty magazines that Davey Beam had swiped from his older brother's room.

The three of us – Davey, Curtis Jefferies and I – were the last the original kids our age who'd moved onto Walker in 1977. We'd played together like all the kids on the street, but never really became friends. Yet, it was clear to all of us we weren't going anywhere, so we just sort of looked out for each other. Movers came to other houses over the years but never to ours.

Davey's family could afford to get away from Walker but they stayed. I'm not sure why. We didn't talk about stuff like that. But the day after Curtis thirteenth birthday, his parents were killed in a car accident and he was sent to live with an aunt and uncle in the city. We never saw him again.

As I grew older and traded pick-up hockey games, baseball cards and pictures of half-naked women for a part-time job at the music store downtown, I stopped thinking about life on Walker altogether. It was what it was.

By the time I was nineteen, I'd found an assembly line job rolling cigarettes, for thirteen bucks an hour – great money for a kid with nothing more than a high school education. Our little house had faded from yellow to a dirty-beige over the years. Inside, things never changed. That year, I moved out and never looked back.

Leaving Ron and Gertie was easy. They weren't good parents. Ron was away most of the time. When he was home, his nights consisted of little more than relaxing in his chair with his feet up to watch TV, barking at the younger kids to change the channel or fetch him another beer. Gertie, well, I'd already told you she wasn't much of a mother. Leaving her probably extended my life. But leaving Dale, Jason and Cherie was harder than I thought it would be. I loved them in my own way, but they didn't have much to say to me.

The only time I remember feeling like someone in my family loved me was the day I left. Cherie was standing in the middle of the street, in bare feet, wearing a little pink sundress, wailing as I disappeared down Walker with a backpack and my bike.

"THOMAS!!!!!!!!" she screamed. "Don't go."

Once I'd rounded the corner, I stopped. I let my bike fall to the sidewalk and crept up to the side of the last house on the street. It had belonged to so many families over the years I didn't know who even lived there anymore. I pressed my back against the side of the house and peered around the corner. Cherie's crying had stopped, but she was still standing in the street looking about as lost as I knew she felt. For a moment, I wanted to go back for her. I wanted to pick her up and hug her and tell her everything would be OK. But I'd be lying, and we didn't really do hugging and loving well in our family. I didn't really know what lay ahead for me or for any of them. I hoped they'd all get out as soon as they could, but there was a part of me that wondered if things could go back to normal without me around. Or, maybe our family was just too far gone.

Dale was smart. He was probably the smartest of any of us kids. He could get loans and grants and scholarships and go to school some-where far away from Walker. Jason might make his way to a community college if he worked hard enough. He still had a few years to think about it and he'd just gotten a job at the pizza place by the high school. His marks were decent enough and if he could scrape the money to-gether he'd get a diploma. Cherie was still young. But, with no one looking out for her, chances were she'd be pregnant by the time she was sixteen. Probably, she'd be knocked up by some deadbeat like Ron.

I picked up my bike and pedalled away.

I paid $100 every month for a room in the basement of a house with a few other guys. It wasn't anything special – just a couple of rooms at opposite ends, with a bathroom and a living room in the middle. There was a microwave and a sink but no stove. There were only two bed-rooms but four of us lived there. Each room was divided in half with a curtain. We worked different shifts at the same factory, but didn't hang out much, even when we were all home. Tony and Gino were friends from high school. They kept to themselves – often staggering home in the evenings, reeking of cheap beer and weed. And, Matt had a girlfriend. When she wasn't behind his side of the curtain, he was at her place.

The landlord had given me the room on the condition that I "leave those boys to themselves." They tolerated me living there, but like being at home, the guys just didn't like me much.

I spent a lot of time alone. I tried for more shifts at the factory, but older workers got most of the extra-shifts and overtime. So, I bought a used ghetto blaster from the thrift store down the street to drown out my thoughts. It had a dual cassette deck so I bought a couple of tapes that people were starting to ditch in favour of compact discs. But the music bothered the family upstairs. Over and over, they told me to turn down the volume. And, I did, but not for long. Without the noise, the silence was unbearable. On Walker, I'd had the neighbourhood din to fill my headspace. Screaming kids, traffic, moving trucks, Ron and Gertie cursing at each other, the constant noise from Ron's TV, the rumble of a passing train; it provided a soundtrack. The background noise stopped me from thinking about things, which is probably why I'd survived as long as I had.

Being on my own was different than I imagined. I thought I'd be able to be myself, make something of a better life – and be happy. But, for a kid from the north-end, with little education, no real skills and friends, it was no better than living on Walker. It might have even been worse. When the gossip swirled about me, there was nowhere and no way to hide from it.

For months, I tried to make a go of it. I tried to be as normal as I could. But, with nothing to throw myself into beyond twelve hour shifts at the factory, I felt more alone than ever.

And then I met Kate. She worked nights at the 7-11. When I finished my afternoon shifts I would often stop in there to grab a Big Gulp. I hadn't noticed her until she made a point of asking my name one Thursday night.

"I see you in here a lot," she said as she handed me my change.

I nodded without looking up at her, stuffed the money in my pocket and turned to go, but she kept talking. "I bet you work over at the tobacco factory, huh?"

I nodded again, feeling the need to leave but not wanting to be rude. She was the first person to acknowledge my existence in months.

"I'm Kate."

"Thomas," I mumbled.

"OK," she said. "Well, Thomas, it's very nice to meet you. Maybe I'll see you in here again."

The next night, I almost didn't go in. I wasn't looking for any company in my life, but the emptiness was painful. But I went in that night...and Kate and I became friends. I'd never really had one before. I'd hung out with Davey and Curtis because of proximity and circumstance, but Kate was choosing to get to know me. It was exhilarating and unsettling all at the same time. I shared bits of my life on Walker because she asked, but I never told her about Gertie or Ron. I knew it was just a matter of time before she started asking questions about them and I worried our friendship might not survive if I told her.

One night, Kate was working her usual night shift. I'd just clocked out. I pushed open the door to the 7-11 and the little bell chimed above my head. Kate was at the register. Her hair was deep red and pulled into a ponytail that hung down her back. She was wearing a green company t-shirt.

There were two other customers. A woman in the far corner was looking at cold drinks, oblivious to anyone else, and a well-dressed man, a little older than me, stood next to the register. He wasn't buying anything.

I was starting to let my guard down with Kate, something I'd never been able to do with anyone, but looking at her that night, with this man, made me panic. I turned to leave but Kate called name.

"Thomas!"

I had one hand on the door. My heart raced. And I knew. I was a lot of things – broken, damaged, wounded – but not stupid. I knew what she thought of me. I stood there, frozen, for what seemed like an eternity.

"Thomas?" she called again.

I had to decide now. I had to think. I had to do the thing I had spent my whole life being forced not to do. Panic sprang up in me. I felt ready to erupt. In one moment everything I'd been taught, everything I'd been told to believe about myself, everything that had been drilled into my head growing up about who I was – what I was – bubbled up. Did everyone know? Could everyone see through me?

I knew I should push the door open and run. But what would I be running to? Emptiness? Loneliness? The same hollow, painful life I'd been leading for twenty years? A life filled with wounding thoughts whenever I was in silence. I took my hand off the door and let it fall to my side.

I turned. Kate was smiling at me.

"Come here, Thomas," she said. "I want you to meet Christopher."

I trudged to the counter. I was afraid to look up. My hands shook and I could feel sweat forming at my brow. Christopher extended his hand.

"It's nice to meet you," he said. "Kate's been telling me about her handsome and mysterious friend for a while now."

I froze again. This wasn't right.

My mind raced. Kate had never mentioned Christopher. Why hadn't I heard of him before? Who was this man? Why had they been talking about me?

No, this wasn't right.

In my head I could hear Gertie's biting words being uttered – about me. I heard her again scream at Ron, about me. "He's abnormal, Ronald. It's not right. I won't have that in my house. I will not ac-knowledge that freak. What are people going to think?"

My head started spinning. There was no music playing. The woman by the cold drinks was gone. A light flickered overhead. My mouth went dry.

Another of Gertie's terrible rants about me filled my mind. "I gotta live in this God-forsaken house 'cause there's nowhere else in this town that we can go."

Gertie's words were fresh in my head – they stabbed me now as sharp as when I first heard them twelve years ago. "Ignore him," Ger-tie screamed at my siblings. "You don't want to be catching what he's got. He's not right."

This wasn't right. This wasn't right.

144

I turned and ran, knocking over a display as I pushed through the glass door. I ran across the street, not looking where I was going as car horns blared around me and lights flashed every which way. I screamed. The thoughts in my head were pounding like caged wild animals trying to escape. I couldn't think. I couldn't see. I just ran.

And then I heard it. The whistle of the train. I knew from the deafening sound that it was close. I could feel the vibration start to shake the ground and the light come into view. I didn't have much time to think. I didn't want to think, but Gertie's words couldn't be silenced by the roar of the engine.

"You are not a girl. You are a boy. A sick, strange, twisted, weird little boy. You were born a boy and you will always be a boy. I will kill you, child, if you ever breathe a word of this to anyone."

And then the noise was gone.

Wife. Mother. Woman of faith. Imperfect human being. Kathleen Elliott swapped a journalism career in 2004 for the gift of raising her two young sons. She now works in the communications sector in the Guelph area. She was a reporter/photographer at the *Guelph Mercury* from 1998-2004.

George Goes to Dinner

Greg Mercer

George Rumple frowned deeply and eased himself into the tufted, wingback chair at the end of the dining room table. It was an overly luxurious chair for eating a meal, he thought. He pretended to sip his wine, vaguely mad at his hosts. Carl, wearing a yellow golf shirt stretched around his ample stomach, beyond the reasonable limits of fabric, hadn't stopped talking since he'd arrived.

"Mary and I go to Florida every winter. You'd love it," Carl said, in between great jabs at the bloodied chunks of beef on his plate. The last grey wisps of hair clinging to his massive head had been brushed across to the top of his scalp and appeared held in place with some sort of glue.

"It would be good for you, you know, a change of scenery. Must be awful being in that house all alone, with all those memories. And it sure beats the heck out of shovelling the driveway."

George, in fact, didn't mind the winter. The cold season in his part of the country was not as severe as in other northern regions. It snowed, sometimes frequently, but rarely enough to prevent him from retrieving the newspaper on the walkway. Besides, he enjoyed using his Mastercraft snow-blower, preferably at 5:00 a.m., before the sun rose, just to show his neighbours what a responsible homeowner he was.

"I'm fine here in Wallaceburg," George said.

That prompted Carl, still chewing, to get into a long discussion of the buffet restaurants to be had in Florida, and their mountains of shrimp, roast beef and crab legs for the taking. He nodded his head approvingly and patted his generous belly as he talked.

"They've got this one place in Clearwater where it's all you can eat chicken wings. Now, if you go on Tuesdays, it's half price. That's $9. If you eat eighteen wings, it works out to just 50 cents a wing. But I usually eat more than that. I'll skip lunch and go good and hungry, and really get my money's worth."

"One time, he ate forty chicken wings! We counted," Mary added, putting her fork down.

Carl nodded and pursed his lips.

"And they've got all the flavours. Even kinds we can't get up here. Buffalo-style, Cajun, honey garlic, smoky barbecue. It has mesquite in it. Have you ever seen a place around here offer smoky barbecue chicken wings? They're quite ahead of us down there, when it comes to stuff like that. They're very advanced."

George started counting spiral patterns in the ceiling stucco.

"They've got all the best places down there. The Barbecue Barn, China Palace, Sea King Buffet –"

"East Side Mario's," Mary said.

"That's not a buffet place," Carl said, irritated. He jammed another forkful of broccoli into his mouth and continued. "Oh, and you've got to try this place, Golden Corral. Steaks, shrimps, seafood, you name it. Potatoes cooked five different ways. They're mostly a steak place, though."

"If you leave Golden Corral hungry, there's something wrong with you," Mary added, helpfully.

"And this is very important: if you go, you've got to go at ten after four. Because that way they still charge you the lunch price, but at 4:30 they start switching over to the dinner. They bring out the steaks and the shrimp then, but you're allowed to eat it. And you save $3 that way. But don't let them try to sell you a drink. That just adds to the price. That's how they make their money."

There were 22 stucco spirals going the width of the room, George observed. He began counting them length-wise, with an eventual plan to do the math and obtain the total number of stucco spirals.

"There's a breakfast place in St. Pete's," Carl continued."Moe's? No Mory's. No, it's –"

"Isn't it called Maurice's?" Mary suggested.

Carl shook his head.

"That's in Dunedin. The little place by the marina. No, this place is called Moe's, right off the I-64 as you're coming into St. Pete's. They've got all these old movie posters on the walls. This Moe's place, they do an all-day breakfast for $2.99. They'll try to get you by asking if you want coffee, but that's $2.25, so right there your meal cost is almost doubled. What I do is I'll make a pot at the trailer before we head out, so I don't need any at the restaurant. Then I'll just order a water with my breakfast, which of course is free."

Thirty-one stucco spirals going the length of the dining room. That made 682 spirals, George reckoned. No, that didn't make sense. He began doing the math again, while Carl began a discussion of the all-you-can-eat grouper nights at the fish fry restaurants in Clearwater.

After dinner, they moved to the living room where George sat alone, expressionless on the middle cushion of a pale green chesterfield. Mary and Carl each took a coral-pink armchair facing George, who felt like he was at a job interview. He tried to remember to sit up straight. Carl started explaining his theory on why the Tigers were losing the lead in late innings when a left-handed pitcher was on the mound. George nodded politely, holding his warm glass of wine with both hands, not a drop missing. When Mary left the room a few minutes later, Carl leaned forward and started whispering.

"George, there's another reason to go to Florida. You've gotta see the women," he said, then proceeded to spread both hands palm upward in front of his chest and slowly bounced them up and down like he was holding something heavy.

"What are you doing? Is something wrong with your hands?" George asked.

Carl bounced his hands in front of his chest more emphatically, then nodded seriously, as if that proved his point. He squinted at his friend on the chesterfield.

"I don't understand," George said.

"Those girls have got a figure," Carl whispered, squinting harder now. "Figures like you've never seen around here."

Mary returned to the room with a plate of gingersnap cookies and a half-empty bottle of wine. Carl motioned for his glass to be topped up.

He took a fistful of the hard, round treats and resumed his discussion of the Tigers' bullpen. George enjoyed talking baseball, but Carl's dissertations on the game always managed to lead their way back to his own playing days. An hour later, the sun had dropped out of sight and Carl had changed the topic from the Detroit Tigers to the closure of the Ford plant ten years earlier, and finally to his own career as a pitcher, which was unjustly stopped short in high school because of a torn tendon. Carl said the injury came from throwing too hard.

"They said I was just too strong for my own good," Carl said.

George quietly wondered if the injury was perhaps related to a pulled jaw muscle. After the scrapbook came up from the basement, showing black and white pictures of Carl as a young man, standing in a baseball uniform with a wispy moustache, his guest decided it was time to leave. George carefully placed his wine glass on the coffee table, took a deep breath and slowly clutched at his chest. He grimaced, mildly at first, then more severely, wincing as if he was sitting on a tack. Carl didn't look up from the scrapbook and began showing his wind-up motion that he used as a teenager. George grabbed at his chest more violently, flapping his right arm against his leg as if it were possessed. Still Carl didn't look up. George began shaking and popping his eyes out of his head as best he could, for effect. Now Carl was standing, but pretending he was trying to pick off the runner at first base. He threw over to the imaginary first baseman. George advanced his demonstration a step further, emitting what he intended to come out like a groan that ended up sounding more like a gurgle.

"George, are you alright?" Mary said, finally coming into the room and noticing him. "Oh my goodness, Carl! Help!"

At that moment, George's eyes began to roll back in his head and he fell sideways onto the couch, clutching at his collar, a performance that may fairly be described as a touch too melodramatic but effective nonetheless. Within twenty minutes, the Papideaus had taken George to the emergency room of the Wallaceburg General Hospital, where he was promptly wired up to a heart monitor and left sitting on a firm bed.

Strangely, after a battery of tests, the medical staff could find no evidence George was having cardiac arrest, or any other heart problem. His heart beat on, like a marching drum, inside his chest. The nurse suggested he might be suffering from indigestion and sent him home with a prescription for antacid tablets.

"I knew Mary put too much garlic in the mashed potatoes," Carl declared, as they left hospital.

Lost and Found

Phil Andrews

She noticed it right away.

It wasn't a coin.

It was some kind of medallion. A religious one. She wondered if it was worth anything.

Maybe it was silver.

Danny would know. She would take it to him, she thought, as she stared at the thin, smooth thing that a stranger had dropped into her cupped hands – along with three quarters, a nickel and loonie.

It had a pressing of an angel on one side. Very simple. Like something a grade schooler would draw. It was close to a stick-figure. The face was blank. The features were bare. But there were unmistakable wings sprouting above the shoulders of the figure. And, above its head floated a plain oval bubble; its halo. On the reverse, in all-caps, over three lines, was stamped ALWAYS WITH YOU.

She tried to hold a picture in her mind of the woman who had given it to her.

She was short. With dark hair. And freckles on her nose. Dark brown eyes too.

Their eyes had met for a moment. The woman had looked at her after she'd stopped and returned to her – at the foot of the stairs at the subway station, where she'd been mewling for handouts.

"Have you any spare change"

"Have you any spare change?"

"Have you any spare change?"

That's what she called out. Repeatedly. From that spot and a few others, where she placed herself, each afternoon rush hour, until a Toronto Transit Commission security staffer eventually appeared and ushered her away. Usually with gentle grace. And, sometimes not. Not at all.

She had been installed at her St. Patrick's Station perch when the young woman suddenly reappeared before her.

"I have some change for you," she said.

Then, she dropped the pinch of what seemed like coins into her palms, looked at her, then turned away to catch the approaching subway.

She had seen her pass by her before, without seeming to take note of her. She wondered what had made her stop this day. And, what had she meant in passing on this dull, worn angel coin.

It reminded her of the foster family she had lived with for a period as a girl. The Farrells. They had taken her to church every week and sent her to Catholic school too, even though her real mom had never been part of that church. Nor any other.

* * * * *

She only noticed it an hour or so later.

She was going to get out of the jeans she had worn and into tights to go for a run. She emptied her pockets at the counter near the toaster in her kitchen – where she always did. Out came a Chapstick tube. Out came a key to her apartment's basement storage locker. And, out came a quarter. That was all.

She reached back into the pocket feeling for it. Nothing. Then, she tried the other pockets, knowing even as she did that it was pointless. It wasn't there.

Somewhere she had lost the angel medal her mother had given to her. She had received it when she left home to go to U of T three years before.

She had never really been without it since getting it. It had significance upon receipt of it. It represented her mom, a reminder of that dear, unstinting booster of hers and a tiny reinforcement of the faith her family held. She had turned that medallion over and over in her hands countless times. It was a charm. It was more. It helped her many times when she felt anxious, alone or far from home. And, now it was missing.

She checked the pocket she was sure had held it feeling this time for a hole. But there was none.

Then, it struck her. She had given it away. She had given it to that woman. The one in the subway. She had always felt terrible slipping past her. But it always seemed there was a subway train just coming into the station when she was planted at the stairs, so close to the landing where the subway train's doors briefly swooshed open and closed.

She had vowed many times to hand her some money – the next time.

Not today though. Today, she U-turned and returned to the woman after hustling to the platform and noting a train was just slipping away. She reached into her pocket for some coinage as she did.

"I have some change for you," she'd said.

The panhandler had turned at the statement and the women faced each other. The woman let the donation tumble into the other's hands and took a step back – without assessing what she had provided.

"Thank you," said the begging woman. She ended the moment between them abruptly, returning to make more requests of others descending the stairs towards her.

The woman finished changing for her run as she thought about the exchange and about inadvertently gifting the medal to the woman.

"Dammit," she whispered, as she headed out to get in her jog.

* * * * *

"It's not silver. My guess is that it's pewter," said Danny, as he turned the object over in his yellow-stained fingers.

He picked at the angel effigy with his long thumbnail.

"I'll pawn it and see what you get," he told Cathy.

"I...I don't know. If you don't think it's worth anything much, maybe I'll just keep it," Cathy said, reaching out for the keepsake.

She had started to think about holding on to it even if Danny had said it was solid silver.

"Whatever. It's probably like about five bucks for one. New," said Danny, handing it over to his sometimes girlfriend. "I'd rather have gotten a toonie."

Cathy wasn't so sure. Since she first stared at the thing, she felt pleased to have it. She felt strangely comforted by it – though she wasn't a church person or into angels or anything like that.

She figured the woman who gave it to her did it as a message. Something more than a handout. Maybe she was some kind of church worker. Not a crackpot. A harmless one. She was sure of that.

* * * * *

She was sure it was gone. It was probably traded or sold or tossed by the woman shortly after she had come to possess it.

But she decided to ask about it, when she next saw the woman. That would be something for bystanders to observe: someone seeking a coin from the woman begging for them in the subway station.

She would offer her money for it.

Maybe $10. She didn't want it to appear like the angel coin was worth a lot of money and it probably wasn't at all. But she thought the gesture of offering some money in exchange for it would help – after she explained things and asked for the return of the medal.

Oh, it was going to be awkward. But, whatever. She would feel better to have the angel-coin again. She at least had to try.

As luck had it, the woman was back at St. Patrick's Station, at rush hour, the very next afternoon.

She heard her bleat: "Have you any spare change?" before she saw her.

She fumbled to get at her wallet, in her purse, as she stepped amid a crowd walking down the stairs. She hugged the purse to her chest as she opened the wallet to where it stored bills, well, a bill. All she had was a $20 bill. She hadn't bargained on offering that much. And, yet it was in her hand as she came to be arms-length away from the woman as she repeated her familiar call.

"Have you any spare..."

The handout-seeker broke off her ask as she took in the woman before her holding a twenty.

She stood with a palm cupped for receipt of coins and her other hand closed in a ball at her side.

"I have to thank you; for this," she said.

And, as she did, she raised her fist from her side, turned and opened the hand and revealed the medal. She had been holding the medal. The ALWAYS WITH YOU side was showing.

"I'm happy you like it," said the university student.

She then placed her twenty on the coin.

"Have a good day," she uttered softy. Then, she scuttled to pass through the open doorway of the subway train which had just come to rest at the edge of the platform.